The Code of the
Zombie Pirate

The Code of the Zombie Pirate

HOW TO BECOME AN UNDEAD MASTER OF THE HIGH SEAS

Scott Kenemore

Illustrations by Matt Meyer

Skyhorse Publishing

Skyhorse Publishing books may be purchased in bulk at special discounts for sales promotion, corporate gifts, fund-raising, or educational purposes. Special editions can also be created to specifications. For details, contact the Special Sales Department, Skyhorse Publishing, 555 Eighth Avenue, Suite 903,
New York, NY 10018 or info@skyhorsepublishing.com.

www.skyhorsepublishing.com

10 9 8 7 6 5 4 3 2 1

Library of Congress Cataloging-in-Publication Data is available on file.

ISBN: 978-1-61608-120-1

Printed in Singapore

For Stephanie

Contents

Preface

"He gives us our lives in exchange for living dead."
—Errol Flynn, *Captain Blood*

I.

We are alike, we zombies and pirates. We are alike because we want the same things.

We want to inspire fear and terror in the innocent, law-abiding populace.

We want to disrupt commerce—whether it's intercontinental shipping routes or just the Cinnabon stand at the local shopping mall.

We want to kill and wreak havoc generally, but we also want to recruit others—select others—to join our own ranks.

We don't respect political barriers or legal documents.

We are hunted by armies, navies (maybe especially navies), and all manner of members of the law enforcement community. We can expect no quarter from our foes. (In truth, we can usually expect to be killed on sight.) We will give no quarter in return.

We are universally detested. Upon sight, our presence brings cries of alarm. Whenever we show up, people understand that something is very, **very** wrong.

And yet . . .

We delight in what we do. That can be the only word for it. **Delight.** Despite the foes ranged against us, we never hesitate or entertain a second thought about our chosen vocation. We never doubt ourselves. We are zombies. We are pirates. This is who we are. This is what we *have* to be doing.

II.

You are an ambitious dreamer, as anyone can see. You occupy your mind with only the highest, most noble pursuits.

Power. Wealth. Expansion of your territory and the ability to bend others to your will.

You don't need this book to tell you that **zombies and piracy are two of the most expeditious routes to realizing these desires.**

Who has not dreamed of harnessing the awesome power of a voodoo priest and using it to create an army of zombies?

Who has not contemplated—sometimes with a desperate intensity—the many treasures of the Caribbean that could be easily taken . . . if only one had the will . . . and the means?

And who can honestly say they have not dreamed of a life on the high seas as a pirate king or queen?

These things are not merely the distractions of a daydreamer. To the contrary, they are all within your grasp. They are real, achievable objectives. Others have obtained them, so why not you?

It is not your *worthiness* that determines whether you shall have a life of a penurious servitude or be knee-deep in ducats before you're thirty. (How many of the rich people you know really seem to be *worthy* of their wealth and stature?) Neither are forthrightness, hard work, education, piety, or attendance at tedious "social networking" events prerequisites for a life of success and plunder.

All that you really need is a guide. Or, more precisely, a code . . .

III.

Though they are often incorrectly stereotyped as beings that are entirely lacking in self-control, if you look closely you will find that both zombies and pirates adhere to stringent codes of conduct that govern almost every aspect of their lives (or, in the case of zombies, "lives").

Zombies, for example, never attack other zombies. Zombies are careful never to sleep, rest, or dawdle. Zombies accept all other zombies into their ranks, regardless of creed, skin color, sex, or national origin. Zombies attack all humans, whenever and wherever it's possible to do so. Zombies do not speak about topics other than brains.

Pirates also live by strict codes that govern their behavior. (Remember, just because it allows for plundering, woman-izing, and a lifestyle of constant violence, doesn't mean it's not still a code.) Pirates are not allowed to attack others in their crew. Pirates agree that the more experienced, higher-ranking pirates shall get a greater share of any captured treasure. Pirates agree not to leave a pirate ship—and the captain not to disband a crew—until each pirate aboard has accumulated an amount of money determined before they set sail.

Both zombies and pirates have codes they follow. Awesome, incredibly permissive, violence-centric codes, but codes nonetheless. Is this the reason zombies and pirates are so cool? Quite possibly. Zombies are cool and pirates are cool, but I am here today to propose something greater than both. Namely, that it is by **combining zombies with piracy** that optimum financial success can be achieved.

By sailing the seven seas (or, really, just the Caribbean) with a brain-eating crew of the undead, the wildest daydreams of even the most avaricious pirate can be realized. The benefits of a zombie pirate crew (over, say, a human crew that will want things like food and water and a share of the treasure) are as diverse as they are substantial. The Caribbean is a mystical place, filled with charms and magic and voodoo. It's also a murderous, lawless place. The dead are already all around you, and they're just begging to be reanimated for a second life of piracy.

As the captain of a ship filled with zombie pirates, you will enjoy benefits and advantages that will put you head and shoulders above the other "regular" pirates. You will succeed where others fail. The ducats (and crowns, and dollars, and giant gold bars) will come rolling in.

A project of such unparalleled scope and ambition as zombie piracy requires more than a simple ten- or fifteen-item checklist of "dos and don'ts." The Zombie Pirate Code contained in this manual provides the in-depth study of the practices and tendencies that you need to understand if you are to become a successful zombie pirate captain.

Make no mistake about it. Zombies are hard to kill, but they are not invincible. Pirates laugh in the face of laws that govern other men, but many are captured and hanged for doing so. Without a strong sense of direction and rules to follow, a zombie pirate captain can be just as lost as a zombie wandering through a blasted apocalyptic waste-land and just as dead as a pirate hanging from the gibbet (while some wig-wearing colonial governor looks on approvingly).

If you are willing to take your study of this code seriously—and to combine your dreams of plunder and riches with a deep love of the black arts—then limitless horizons present themselves, and the jewels, treasures, and mysteries of the Caribbean shall be yours.

Welcome aboard. The sea and the grave await!

Introduction

The Origins of Zombie Piracy

Bullies. Everybody hates them, but it takes a special kind of person to **do something about them.** A special person like **you.**

After all, you were just minding your business, weren't you? You were just living here in the coolest part of the world, a place named after the Carib Indians because they were the biggest badasses anybody had ever seen. They spent all their time attacking people and *eating* them. (A little like zombies, if you think about it . . .) But you were coexisting with the Caribs, cultivating awesome religions like voodoo, and cooking your food in wooden barbeque pits called

boucan fires. (This latter trait—believe it or not—was the most distinctive thing about you, such that the Europeans passing through began to refer to you as "buccaneers.")

The Europeans . . . the **bullies.**

At first they seemed friendly . . . not like stupid, mean bullies at all. They came over on pretty ships, brought goods to trade, and were excited to meet everybody and explore everything. Sure, they had some asinine ideas about

Christianity being the one true faith and how they were going to find a city of gold and/or a fountain of youth out in the jungle somewhere, but what're you gonna do, right? No sense in dashing their hopes. They seemed so earnest and serious about it all. Best to just let them tire themselves out. "I know one little conquistador who's going to sleep good tonight," right? (Conquistadors always say they're not tired when they're the **most** tired . . .)

Then, suddenly, **they changed.** They stopped flitting about and searching for gold buildings and spouting here and there about Jebus. They got focused and mean. They figured out what they wanted, and it was all your best shit. Your best land. Your resources. Your women. Your money. And they wanted to just take it. And there were a bunch of them, and they had a bunch of guns and swords.

What did **you** do? Did you give up and roll over? Did you agree to their "requests" that you forfeit your land and pay tributes to foreign powers? Turn your neighborhood into part of a subservient colony? Go down without a fight?

Hell no.

You took to the seas. You armed your ships until they were as mighty as any of the European naval vessels. You roamed the land and sea . . . (like a pirate, yes, but also like a zombie). You preyed upon the soldiers who had taken your land and the land of your kinsmen. You preyed upon the European merchants who sought to exploit you. You preyed upon the religious officials who had sought to convert you. You were murderous. You were merciless. Your reputation grew. (Soon, "buccaneer" stopped meaning "those island people with quaint barbecuing practices," and started meaning "those island people who are roaming the seas and fucking killing us all night and day.")

And while many of your cohorts stopped there—figuring that a policy of man-made murder and plunder was, you know, good enough—**you** saw that a deeper, more profound resistance was possible. **You** aspired to **something greater.**

Your colleagues in piracy might have seen fit to man their ships with fellow island-dwelling barbecue enthusiasts, but you understood that doing so eliminated using another key asset of the Caribbean.

On an island the Spanish arrogantly named Hispaniola, residents had long been animating the dead with a powerful magic called voodoo. (Yes, all right . . .) Or "voudun," or "Vodun," or "voodoun." (Happy now? May I continue?) Parts of it might have come from Africa or other cool places. Nobody seemed to be 100 percent sure. There was consensus, however, on the fact that it was **totally awesome.** You, with great foresight, understood that, however it was spelled, voodoo could be combined with piracy to decimate the Europeans and send them packing.

The bodies reanimated through voodoo were not simply alive again. They were **suggestible.** They could be commanded, like obedient automatons. They were the ultimate soldiers a general might wish to command on the battlefield. They would charge blindly into certain destruction if so ordered. They could withstand punishing damage and only seemed to be "killed" when their heads were destroyed or separated from their bodies. They required no pay, food, or sleep, and were content to let you do all the thinking for them.

Then, as time went by, zombies seemed to evolve. They retained their slow, automaton-like movements—but where they had previously required a prompt to, say, go on a murderous rampage of mayhem and carnage, they began to develop an innate taste for human flesh. (And **brains.** Brains seemed to be the very best of all. . . .) Zombies seemed to want to attack and eat humans on their own, of their own volition, **just because they liked it.** This could, of course, prove problematic when the wrong persons were attacked.

It soon became clear that it would take a special kind of person to manage these zombies and that it would take a **very special** kind of person to employ zombies in the buccaneer's trade. He or she would have to find a way to keep the zombies in line and make sure that their murderous, brain-eating "efforts" furthered the cause of the mission at hand. However, astute pirate captains wagered that cultivating a zombie crew—though a difficult task, certainly—would be well worth the effort.

No surer engine of plunder, adventure, and pure, unadulterated awesomeness exists than a ship of zombie pirates. What an exhilarating joy to be captain of a rotting crew of brain-eating representatives of the living dead! To smell the briny sea air intermingled with the rot of decaying human flesh! To bedeck oneself in stolen jewels! To live! (In . . . a manner of speaking.) A zombie captain will enjoy power, adventure, and unrivaled glory. He or she will amass great wealth, and international reputation. His or her crew will be the envy of the seas.

And so . . .

If you think you're man—or woman—enough for the task, the Code of Zombie Piracy contained in this book will provide a step-by-step guide to the art of plundering with the undead. You will learn how to create/recruit an army of zombies ready to sail the high seas, find a seaworthy vessel appropriate for your nefarious practices, and set sail in pursuit of treasure, plunder, and fucking up those stupid, arrogant, mean European bastards who took all your shit.

It will not always be an easy life. All pirates are hunted as much as they themselves hunt. When word gets back to the mainland of an ass-kicking ship of the dead, attacking ships regardless of the colo(u)rs they fly and eating the brains of the captured, people around the world are going to be gunning for you every chance they get. **Make no mistake:** A zombie pirate captain is wanted dead or alive by every nation and pursued at every turn. Traps will be laid for you. The best and brightest of the world's navies will trail you. Bounties will be offered for your head (preferably, disconnected from the rest of your body).

Should this dissuade you from an awesome and kick-ass life of zombie piracy? By no means.

Should you be ready for it? Absolutely.

That's exactly what the code contained in the book will do: completely prepare you for the trials you're about to face.

I'm ready if you are.

Let's begin.

Deciding What Kind of Zombies (and What Kind of Pirates) You Want to Command

I won't sugarcoat it. This first part is going to be a bit of work. What can I say? Things are tough out here.

It's hot. It's the early 1700s. Lawlessness abounds. European navies are sailing around like a bunch of jerks—they think they're so cool with their bright flags, fancy-lad uniforms, and weevil-free biscuits. Commerce and shipping are profitable, true, but unless you're aligned with a European superpower or a major shipping conglomerate, no one cares a spit about you out here. For the Average Joe, it's hard just getting a boat to ferry you from island to island.

You constantly have to worry about dying of tropical diseases. (If you **do** get sick, doctors will just put leeches on you and bleed you until you die.) It's a million goddamn degrees every day, but for some reason, prudence and decorum dictate that you must walk around in trousers and a doublet. People still use swords—fucking swords!—for fighting. There are guns, yes, but they're accurate at about the same distance as the length of a sword. Also, shoot a gun once, and you need to stop and reload it—a process that takes about two minutes **if you're fast and good at it.** (This is why pirate captains carry like ten pistols stuck into every crevice of their bodies. Ten pistols are ten shots. Chances are, you've got way, way more than ten people to kill, so it's not a perfect solution by any means . . .) There are also cannons, which are far more accurate than pistols—especially seeing as they're usually shot from ships at other ships in coordinated broadside attacks. Nobody just carries around a cannon.

On the plus side . . . well, there's rum. Lots and lots of rum. Armies give it out as part of rations. Doctors prescribe it for anything and everything. (Think: pharmaceutical lobby of 2010 = rum lobby of 1700.) Nine times out of ten, getting a nice rum buzz on is going to be the only thing that makes your waking life bearable. (You can forget about iPods, air-conditioning, and the Internet).

This part of the world is wild. Unsettled. Dangerous. Maybe there are dragons. Maybe there are cities of gold. Nobody really knows yet. Given this pervading sense of "anything could happen here," the Caribbean tends to attract adventure-seekers and people looking to get rich quick. Sure, there will be a sprinkling of religious zealots, uninteresting locals, and stoic government officials, but, by and large, the Caribbean is not a place where boring people come. It's interesting, and so are most of the people who choose to live in it. It's a place where fortunes are made or lost. Where a man can be a criminal one day and a pirate king the next. And where a person who knows what he or she wants can take it. With zombies.

Now, like I said, you just have to decide what kind of zombies they're going to be.

Let's start with the extremes. On one end of our spectrum is the traditional, early-stage Haitian voodoo zombie. This zombie is created by a priest or shaman from the corpse of a recently deceased peasant. These zombies are the most common in the Caribbean. They are also the least autonomous, and—let's be honest—the least interesting. Having been reanimated soon after death, voodoo zombies can often be mistaken for living humans—at least from a distance. These zombies are quiet. They speak only when spoken to, and they speak like robots. Boring robots. Sometimes these zombies are employed in situations where they have to impersonate living humans, but the best these zombies can pull off is sounding like a patient with a motor-neural injury. These traditional zombies are content to stand looking at their own shadow for hours on end or to while away a day walking in endless circles. They are also content to commit murder and sow chaos in villages throughout Hispaniola if so ordered . . . **but only if so ordered.** These zombies can do what needs doing, but they also require considerable micromanagement. In a way, these are the slackers of the zombie world. They'll do things if you stand behind them commanding them, but otherwise, they just sort of hang around.

Let's go to the other end of the spectrum. Here, one finds the zombie who comes into being with one thing and one thing only on his mind—eating the minds of others. These zombies generally come into being through deals with Satan, readings from the texts of Abdul Al Hazred, or through the desecration of Indian burial grounds (probably Carib Indians—again, they *really* liked to eat people). These zombies are "born" to kill humans. From the very moment they spring out of the grave, they spend 100 percent of their time attempting to eat people. Often, this proves more easily said than done. For you see, zombies on this *other* extreme may not be recently deceased. Often, they have rotted in the ground for years. Sometimes they are missing limbs, faces, teeth, and other things that are helpful when you want to eat people. Do these physiological setbacks deter these zombies? Not at all. These cannibal zombies—though loath to be commanded or corralled—are ideal to have when the work turns bloody and the enemy is near. With these zombies in his or her crew, a zombie pirate captain will not need to make memorable speeches or grand displays to inspire his minions to attack. These zombies have a default setting of "attack, kill, and eat the enemy." A pirate captain's only concern will be what to do with these zombies when they are **not** needed for close combat.

As you might imagine, a crew of extremes can be extremely hard to deal with. However, a shrewd pirate captain understands that somewhere in between "crew of **unmanageable murderers**" and "crew of automatons who must be **micromanaged constantly**" is a crew of zombie pirates who are up for the hunt and kill, yet still able to take orders now and then. Certainly, you want violent tendencies. I mean, that has to be there. You're not going to go to the trouble to cripple and raid merchant

ZOMBIE TIP:
The Quick and the Undead . . .

You've got to choose one or the other (because zombies usually aren't both), and as a zombie pirate captain, you've got to live with that choice.

vessels so that you can compliment the crew on their haircuts. You're more focused on making them walk the plank and taking their treasure. Violent zombies will make this happen, but you still need the zombies to be subject to your will. You need to be able to call them off when necessary, or have them wait until the moment is right to strike. A zombie pirate who doesn't listen to his pirate captain isn't useful to anybody.

One good way to reach this area of compromise between zombie extremes is to have your local voodoo priest reanimate the cadavers of murderous pirates. Because they've been reanimated through voodoo, these zombies are liable to be of the commandable variety. However, a pedigree of piracy will run through their bones (and rotting sinews, and desiccated muscles), and when the cutlasses and cannonballs start flying, **they'll know what to do.** Just as zombies have a way of remembering artifacts from their former lives when they interact with them—things like umbrellas, door handles, and how to salute—so do zombies have a knack for remembering certain situations. Even a zombie whose senses have been dulled by the voodoo reanimation process will usually have some idea of when it's time to weigh anchor and cruise the seas for prey.

If, however, you find yourself in possession of zombie reanimated through magical or supernatural means—the kind that already want to kill and kill and kill—take heart. All is not lost. In face, these aggressive and difficult-to-manage zombies can be among your strongest assets. They must be used sparingly and carefully corralled onboard, but in the right circumstances, they can become some of your most powerful weapons. For example, if you can launch a few of these uncontrollable killing-machine zombies onto the deck of an enemy ship (possibly with a catapult or some other cool device), then they're going to create a disruption in that enemy crew far more effective and decimating than a barrage of grapeshot. You can dress these zombies in pantaloons and tricorne hats, and they'll basically fit in with the rest of the crew. By the time the enemy figures out what's up with these guys, it'll be far, far too late for them to do anything about it. Finally (as we'll discuss further), you can hide these zombies in your hold and then unleash them when your ship has come into physical contact with an enemy vessel.

In summary, you want to be a "big tent" kind of zombie pirate captain. If a zombie seems like he can be useful to you—or, you know, is even just around and handy—my advice is to give him an audition. Just as the members of human pirate crews will have different personalities, zombie pirate crews also have room for at least *some* variation. Zombies with different styles are fine, as long as they work together toward the common goal. (Murder, plunder, brains, etc.)

It is **your** job to make sure that happens.

The Benefits of Zombie Pirates (Over, Say, Regular Pirates or Regular Zombies)

Don't get me started on "regular" pirates.

Oh sure, *being* a pirate is one thing. It's all "Yo, ho, ho, and a bottle of rum, and when do we get to go on the next murderin', plunderin', womanizin'-spree?"

Being a pirate is fine and dandy.

But *leading* a group of pirates? That's a pain in the ass right there.

Did you ever wonder why pirate captains like Long John Silver and Blackbeard and Captain Kidd have reputations for being such dicks? Trust me, they didn't start out that way. Blackbeard and others of his ilk got to be complete and total bastards for one reason and one reason only. They were called upon to do the impossible: **manage pirates.**

Think about the worst employee you ever saw at the worst job you ever had. Think about their self-centeredness, their inability to be a "team player," their proclivity for physically attacking coworkers whenever they felt like it. Now multiply those traits about a thousand times, and you've got **some** sense of the workplace behavior you find in somebody who wants to be a pirate.

Wait! You're not fucking done yet. Now take that worst-coworker-times-1,000 and multiply him or her by **an entire crew of pirates.** And now imagine **you're** the one who has to get these ADHD, violence-prone, self-centered drunkards to somehow focus and work together. Even a veteran behavioral psychologist would grant that these people are not going to respond to "positive reinforcement" and "disciplinary timeouts." (Also, Ritalin is still like three hundred years away.)

So what's left? Well, as any pirate captain—no matter how initially beneficent—always learns, pirates tend only to respond to the most base, primal motivators. They want gold and plunder, and they want not to die (probably in that order, but hey, it's not hard and fast with these guys). To get regular pirates to do anything, you have to **threaten to kill them** or **reward them with treasure.** Anything less, and it's just one more step toward an ineffective crew that is going to start thinking about how good a mutiny sounds. For a pirate captain seeking to motivate his crew, the "carrot" has to be brimming with gold and jewels, and the "stick" should be the tip of a cutlass or the end of a plank.

The captain of a ship of **zombie pirates** can remain a **totally awesome dude** (or **seriously cool chick**) while still managing a crew effectively and efficiently. Why? Because you don't have to be a violent jerk to get zombies to do what you want them to do.

Zombies are easy to lead, at least compared to pirates. Zombies don't want money. They don't seek fame or fortune. They don't lust for sexual intercourse. Most important for you, zombies don't aspire to be pirate captains themselves, so nobody's gunning for your job. In fact, they don't care **at all** about rank or promotion. (You won't have lickspittles falling all over themselves wanting to be first mate.) Zombies have no egos or career aspirations. They have only an uncontrollable thirst to feast on the flesh of the living. (This is something that, as a pirate captain, you ought to be able to provide them if you're worth your weight in sea salt.) Pull your bark alongside a British merchant vessel or Portuguese caravel, point them in the right direction, and the rest is a cakewalk.

Further—in sharp contrast to conventional, living pirates—zombies are infinitely replaceable. While a pirate captain commanding human pirates might flinch at the cost (both in human life and capital investment) of sending a boarding party to their almost-certain doom against a better-armed foe, the captain of a zombie crew need have no such compunction. When you know the right voodoo shaman or enchanted burying ground, zombies can be replaced with relative ease and at a reasonable price. Also, you can send wave after wave of zombie pirates to be destroyed without any deleterious effect on the morale of the zombie pirates who must follow after them. They will still be willing to fight for the death for you in any situation. This brings me to my next point . . .

Zombies have **complete faith in your judgment.** So what if your last ten voyages ended in ruinous defeat? So what if you've been defeated by European navies so many times that your nickname is "The Bitch of the Seas"? Zombies will not lose **one single ounce** of confidence in your leadership ability, no matter how much of an incompetent starveling you might appear to be (or might actually be). Zombie pirates will always follow you to the ends of the earth (or at least to where there are brains).

Zombies are also stalwart fighters compared to human pirates. As the cannonballs and grapeshot start to fly, you'll be glad to have them on your side. When you employ zombies for piracy, you get a crew that will fight to the "death" every time. Both zombie pirates and regular pirates are fundamentally selfish entities, **but,** for zombies, the selfish motivations are quite simple. Zombies want to kill humans and eat brains. That's it. Regular pirates want a slew of things (plunder, women, fame, blah blah blah), but they also want to not die or be destroyed in the course of getting stuff. Zombies do not have this keep-living-and-not-die "hang-up" appended to their collective psychology. Zombies just go for the gusto. A crew of zombie pirates will not hesitate to attack larger vessels, it will not flee or surrender when the tide of battle (or the literal tide) goes against them, and they will never show "fear" in the traditional sense of the word.

Speaking of fear, perhaps the greatest advantage of commanding a crew of zombie pirates is the amount of fear you will strike in the hearts of your enemies. Regular pirates are, of course, already pretty frightening for merchant ships laden with goods and passengers. Pirates go into battle drunk and singing songs. They don't wear uniforms. They howl like animals and smoke hashish and set their beards on fire. Most terrifyingly of all, pirates don't play by the rules. They recognize the legitimacy of no government or treaty. The captured will live or die on the pirates' whim. Station, title, and wealth will not protect anyone in the presence of a pirate. However, at least pirates are, you know, **human.** They can be (to a point) reasoned with. Propositions like: "If you spare my life I'll lead you to where my treasure is buried" at least have the capacity to be *entertained.* Human pirates have been known to allow captured voyagers to become pirates themselves and "enlist" in the crew (which can be an attractive option when the other choice is walking the plank). Zombie pirates don't dance or cavort as they go into battle—and they certainly don't drink rum—but they have the capacity to inspire a terror even beyond that of a traditional pirate. When a merchant or enemy navy encounters zombie pirates, there are only going to be three possible outcomes—defeat the zombie pirates, outrun the zombie pirates, or get eaten by the zombie pirates. **No other thing is going to happen.** You will not reason with them. You will not bribe them into letting you live. You will not flatter them into submission. It's kill or be killed. **That's it.** And speaking of killing, zombies are also hard-to-kill, tenacious fighters, so suiting up to fight a bunch of zombie pirates is way, way more daunting than getting ready to fight conventional pirates.

Whereas the sound of drunken pirate song (and the sight of a Jolly Roger) rightly inspire fear in merchants and navies alike, it is the wafting stench of charnel earth, the eerie stillness and unflinching focus of a pirate ship **crewed by**

zombies, that inspires the ultimate, cosmic terror in those who behold it.

Also, we've got to look at job performance. Zombies are the ultimate nautical warriors. Zombies are equally effective on land or on the sea. Or **in** the sea. When they're not busy fighting sharks or other awesome things, zombie pirates can walk or swim underwater with relative ease. They can also attack. Whereas human sailors who fall overboard in the course of nautical warfare tend to drop their sabers, get their powder wet, and suddenly focus less on "attacking the enemy" and more on "trying not to fucking drown," zombies who are tossed overboard and fall into the sea simply begin attacking from a new direction. In situations where human pirates will selfishly want a rescue, zombie pirates require no intervention.

One thing to take from all this is that if organizing and running a zombie pirate crew sounds like a lot of work, just stop for a second and think about how hard it would be to run an actual human pirate crew. Suddenly, guys who stumble around and moan for "braaaaains" won't be such a big issue for you.

For these and other reasons, the Code of Zombie Piracy directs that you shall be the only human pirate aboard your ship. From here on out, it's **all zombie.**

Your Ship: Finding a Vessel Worthy of a Bunch of (Un)dead Guys

A boat of some kind. It's what separate pirates from run-of-the-mill highwaymen and kidnappers. It's what will separate **you** from "some dude with a lot of zombies following him."

To be a pirate, you've got to do it **on a boat.**

Are there disadvantages to boats? Sure. The most noticeable disadvantage is that you're crammed into a tiny sailing ship with like fifty other criminals (and/or zombies). Personal space will remain an abstract idea for most voyages, even for a pirate captain, whose quarters—albeit the most luxurious aboard—will still be frustratingly cramped. There are no showers or deodorant, and you're in the tropics and all wearing lots of frilly layers for some reason. Also, boats have tactical limitations. They can only take you places on the water, and it has to be deep. Ships get snagged on shoals and undersea rocks. They're expensive and require constant maintenance to prevent falling apart. Your success in operating one will depend on your ability to do things like "tack leeward," "hoist the mizzen topsail," and other asinine-sounding skill sets. Further, you will have to depend on things like wind and waves being cooperative whenever you want to go somewhere.

> **ZOMBIE TIP:**
> **"I'm on a boat!"**
>
> Remember, for it to count as piracy, it has to happen at sea. Lots of zombies have done lots of cool things on land (e.g., disrupted high school dances, posed threats to national security, annoyed graveyard groundskeeping crews)—but only things done on the water can truly qualify as acts of zombie piracy.

But there are advantages, too.

In 1700 (the year it is, remember?), the middle of the ocean is one of the most isolated places on earth. Once you've loaded your plunder and set sail, it is very, very difficult for somebody to come after you. (They would, themselves, have to purchase and outfit an expensive and hard-to-handle sailing vessel.) The ocean surrounding the New World is big and largely unexplored. You want your ship to disappear? Not hard to do. And suppose some lost fishing boat *does* see you. It'll be *days* before they can notify the proper authorities, and more days before the authorities can send a navy warship after you. In a best-case scenario (for them), they'll be operating on information about where you were a week and a half ago. (Remember that in 1700, pirate ships travel slowly, but information travels **even slower.**)

When it comes to selecting an appropriate vessel, every pirate captain has to think about the unique needs of his or her crew, and this is doubly important for zombie pirate captains. History shows that captains of **nonzombie** pirate crews tend to favor ships that are smaller. (These are often called "sloops" by people who are "down" with sailing terminology, but you don't really need to worry about that.) Smaller ships can go faster than big ones, and can catch up to stupid slow merchant vessels. They can also run away from larger, more heavily armed military ships, and are cheaper and more expendable. If your sloop is destroyed by some well-aimed European cannon fire, you're not out that much money. You and your fellow pirates just swim back to port and buy another one with the gold coins hidden in your socks.

But in other, important ways (involving overall coolness), sloops fucking suck.

They're puny-looking. They only have a couple or three sails. They can't carry as many cannons as big ships (sometimes, sloops have as few as four), and they can't carry as many pirates (or zombie pirates). Those they do carry will feel uncomfortably crowded. The holds aboard sloops aren't very big, so they can't hold as much treasure or zombies (or whatever it is you want to carry around with you).

For these reasons, sloops must not be among your choices for a zombie pirate ship. Yes, some pirates swear by small ships because they can take you places *slightly* faster. So what? You want to get there and start sucking and being puny as soon as possible? Can't wait for it? Real impatient to be the wuss of the seas?

Good. I didn't think so.

While small ships might be fine for traditional pirates, **zombie pirates** want big, giant, awesome-looking ships. Big ships may move more slowly, but they're also more deadly. They carry lots of cannons (like thirty or forty), and lots and lots of crew members. Big, proper ships have a ton of sails, too—like as many as ten sometimes. (Sails are important. The eighteenth century is known as the Age of Sails. This alone should give you a clue as to what a big deal sails are. You want a bunch of them on your ship. They tell other people that you mean business. Sails are the "bling" of the 1700s.)

A zombie pirate ship should, itself, be like a zombie. Zombies move slowly, but they are also widely feared as deadly killers. Zombies will pursue their prey to the ends of the earth. Zombies are easy to evade in the short term, but in the long term they will relentlessly pursue a foe until he is exhausted, cornered, and out of ammunition.

A zombie pirate captain is at his or her best when commanding a massive bark that slowly stalks its prey on the high seas. You want many sails, tons (literally) of

cannon, and a massive hold full of teeth-gnashing zombies who can't wait to be loosed as a boarding party.

Big ships also have big holds, which is important, because yours is going to be tightly packed full of zombies. Where a typical pirate captain would have to delegate space in his ship's hold for provisions, rum, and sleeping quarters, a zombie pirate captain has a crew that doesn't sleep, doesn't drink rum, and likes to find its own food. Thus, any extra room down below has just been freed up for (guess what?) . . . more gibbering, brain-eating zombies!

Also, crow's nests look cool, but are almost useless for the purposes of a zombie pirate. Zombies, you see, are almost universally nearsighted, and placing one on your ship's highest point is more likely to disorient it than help it to scan the horizon for your next target. (If you still want an early warning system of some kind, my advice is to tie a zombie to the bowsprit like an undead masthead. This zombie will always be looking ahead, and whenever he sees something his moans will alert the rest of the ship.)

Finally, when you do purchase your giant hulking ship, it is important not to fixate too much on maintenance. You need to drive that ship like a zombie drives its own body— into the ground (or the sea, as the case may be). A zombie pirate captain is at his or her best when steering a creaking, moldering galleon. The sails may be rent. The winches may need oil. The masts may be falling apart. Yet the integrity and fighting-fitness of the vessel have not been compromised. In fact, pirate ships that look as though they might crumble into the sea at any moment can have tactical advantages, such as inspiring curiosity and awe in the enemy ships they approach. Just as a zombie with a railroad tie through its torso can baffle humans (who tend to say such things as "What the hell? How is he walking toward us with a railroad tie through his torso? Let's wait and see what's up with this guy.") so can a moldering ship baffle nautical onlookers. By the time bystanders who gawk at zombies suddenly realize what's up, it tends to be too late to flee. Same thing with a zombie pirate ship. When a British navy admiral is stunned to glimpse a giant, teetering ship of unknown registry barely able to keep above the waves, he is more likely able to order his men to approach it to "see if they can help" (dumbasses). By the time his gold-trimmed spyglass shows him a deck filled with animated corpses and a Jolly Roger flapping in the breeze, he'll be in range of your cannons.

By selecting an appropriate vessel for piracy, you join an ancient fraternity started thousands of years ago when the first criminally inclined caveman jumped on a floating log and rode it around, clubbing other cavemen and taking their shit. Welcome aboard!

What's in a Name?
(A Lot, So Take Picking One for
Your Ship Seriously!)

Choosing an appropriate moniker for your pirate ship is such an important and nuanced thing that a separate portion of the Code is required for its explicit consideration.

First of all, **all ships have names**—this includes pirate ships, merchant ships, and military vessels. A zombie pirate ship needs a name, too. (If you wanted to be all nonconformist and not name your ship, you could do that, true. But people everywhere would uniformly start calling it some variant of *That One Ship with No Name* since it would be the **only one** like it on the seas.)

Verily, you must name your ship, and you must select a name appropriate to your status as a zombie pirate captain. It is important, when doing this, to consider the climate of ship-naming that already exists in Caribbean piracy. Don't pick your name in a vacuum, without considering others who have named pirate ships before you. Go out into the world and get a sense of the ship names that are already out there. Obviously, you want a name that conveys the fact of your being a tough-as-nails pirate (with a crew of flesh-eating zombies) who isn't to be messed with. However, in the world of Caribbean piracy, this aim is often best achieved through subtlety, innuendo, and even misdirection. Contrary to what you might think, names like *Ass-Kicker*, *Total Pirate Badass*, and *Up Yours, You Stupid European Navies* are not currently in use.

The names of piratical vessels tend to fall into certain key categories that use varying degrees of showmanship and wit to get the point across. Consider the following schools of thought with a keen eye to which one your own personality and tastes might favor.

The Guardedly Badass

Many pirates select names for their ships that are kinda, sorta badass . . . but kinda, sorta **not.** Ship names in this category take a step toward declaring their all-out badassery, but then stop just short. (Perhaps this is done to avoid being considered inappropriately boastful. Nobody knows how the convention got started, but now it's here in full force.) The most famous example in this category is probably Blackbeard's ship, *Queen Anne's Revenge.* "Revenge" is a concept and theme worthy of a murderous bloodthirsty pirate, no doubt, but then there is a woman's name, "Anne," and the word "Queen" added to evoke images of a fancy, frilly female (as opposed to a badass, tobacco-chewing, saber-wielding pirate). *Queen Anne's Revenge* denotes both the traditionally tough and violent idea of revenge combined with the traditionally not-tough notion of being a queen.

Another example in this category is Captain Kidd's ship, *Adventure Galley.* It kinda, sorta sounds badass . . . and it also kinda, sorta sounds like some kind of children's attraction at a fair. "Adventure" is just too wide-open. It could be a totally cool, throat-slitting pirate-type of adventure, or some kind of "Adventure Bible Camp"-type adventure. You just don't know.

If you're determined to use at least **some** form of "tough-guy" wording in the name of your ship, then you ought to consider a name from this school of thought. I advise taking your favorite badass word (skull, hook, zombie, etc.) and pairing it with a word that somehow mitigates or deflates its power (girl, flower, tiara, etc.). *Skull Girl* or *Zombie Tiara* are great names for zombie pirate ships.

The Ironically Lame

Know how, a lot of times, fat guys are called "slim" or "tiny"? It's funny because the opposite is true. Calling a huge guy "tiny" is cute because that's the furthest thing from what he is. Lots of pirates—who are totally fierce killers—choose a name for their ship based upon this very idea. If your ship is the terror of the seas, then giving it a name that suggests the **complete opposite** is kinda cool and funny.

The king of this approach to ship naming is a Caribbean pirate named Edward Low. Low did it **several times** with **several different ships** over the course of his career, assigning his impressive barks such counterintuitive names as *Fancy*, *Rose Pink,* and (wait for it . . .) *Merry Christmas.* That's right, Low named his ship after what is very possibly

the least-threatening greeting in the English language: "Merry Christmas." Another famous pirate, Black Bart (a.k.a. Bartholomew Roberts) also employs this approach to a degree, having given one of his fiercest ships the diminutive moniker *Little Ranger*. And Roberto Cofresí, a pirate from Puerto Rico, sails a schooner unthreateningly named the *Mosquito*.

There is a method to the madness of pirates like Low and Black Bart and Cofresí. Giving your ship a wimpy name says: "I'm such a tough guy that I don't need to assert the fact that I can kick your ass. Actually, I'm so tough that I can assert the opposite. **That's** how tough I am." An ironically lame name also makes people think twice before attacking you, because, hey, it sucks enough when you lose a sea battle, but it sucks even more to have to answer the question: "Say, which ship kicked your ass the other day?" with "The . . . erm . . . *Pretty Kitty*" or "The *Delicate Flower*" or "The *Crochet 4 Ever*." Lose to the wrong ship, and you can end up a fucking punch line in stories other pirates tell in bars.

The Name That Makes Fun of European Royalty

Pirates are outlaws. Pirates don't like Europeans navies or the laws they seek to impose (especially the laws against piracy). Who rules these navies and who makes the foreign policy decisions that determine their actions? European royalty.

What, then, could be more annoying to the blue-blooded, wig-wearing kings and queens of Europe than to have lawless pirates steal their very notions of royalty and having royal blood?

Make no mistake, "pirate kings" and "pirate queens" do rule over their ships in the way kings rule kingdoms. However, there's a reason they don't call themselves "pirate presidents" or "pirate admirals" or "pirate generals." Outlaws of the high seas fancy themselves pirate kings or queens specifically because doing so is the ultimate "up yours" to the royalty-based system of government that has hunted pirates for as long as pirates have existed. And if a pirate chooses to consider himself a kind of "royal," then why should this not also be reflected in the name of his ship?

Several prominent pirates have chosen to elevate the bloodlines of their ships in this way. In addition to the aforementioned *Little Ranger*, Black Bart has several ships that follow this naming convention, including *Royal Fortune* and *Royal Rover*. A Caribbean pirate named Stede Bonnet—who took up piracy for the unassailably awesome reason of wanting to spend less time with his wife—sails a ship called the *Royal James.* (You can sort of also put Blackbeard's *Queen Anne's Revenge* in this category too, since it does mention a queen.)

If you're the kind of pirate who really hates—and I mean **really** hates—the wimpy, effete European monarchs who get to make all the rules, then this is the kind of ship name for you!

The Original Name

This unusual category is especially appropriate to zombie pirates. (The reason why should be momentarily obvious.)

Almost all pirates—unless they are fabulously wealthy and have commissioned the construction of their own pirate ship from scratch—come into ownership of the vessel that will be their "pirate ship" either by purchasing it, stealing it, or taking it from someone by force. In all of these cases, the ship has already been in use and therefore **already has a name.** Most of the time, one of the first things a pirate captain does is rename his new ship. It probably has some stupid, un-piratical name assigned to it by a European navy or shipping corporation—and the new captain wants the name of his or her vessel to reflect the life of crime upon which it is about to embark.

But sometimes . . . just sometimes . . . the pirate captain decides that the coolest thing to do is to keep the name of the ship **exactly the same.**

There is a method to this madness (and/or lack of creativity). It has a startling, demoralizing effect on enemy sailors when they see a familiar, friendly ship approaching theirs—and then, upon closer inspection, realize that it is crawling with bloodthirsty pirates and not at all the same ship now.

Hmmmm. Seeing something that looks familiar, and then realizing that something is very wrong with it. A little like seeing a familiar person who has been turned into a zombie, no? Part of the awesome terror that zombies inflict is that they appear to be living humans—or even to be a *particular* human—right up until the moment you notice they have maggots crawling out of their eyes and their lips have rotted off. Forcing your brain to make that switch between classifying an approaching shape as "Bob, my friendly neighbor" and "the brain-eating, flesh-rending zombie that used to be my neighbor Bob" has an absolutely paralyzing effect on people. Many folks simply can't get over the fact that their former friend or loved one is now a zombie, and so, through their paralysis, are then eaten **by that very zombie.**

Keeping the name of a captured ship the same may not literally paralyze your nautical foes, but it will definitely elicit a strong "What the **fuck**?" reaction when they learn that a formerly friendly bark is now in the possession of murderous pirates.

Several nonzombie pirates have opted for this naming strategy. One, called Henry Morgan (you may know a rum named after him), used it to great success when he came into possession of a top-of-the-line British warship called the *Oxford*. Morgan could have given it some awesome, badass pirate name, but he instead elected to leave it unchanged. This forced those he encountered in battle to go "Oh hey, it's the *Oxford*," and then, moments later, "Oh crap, it's Henry Morgan!"

Considering the zombie-like principle upon which this ship-naming convention rests, it is strongly recommended for zombie pirates. If you like, you can keep the ship's name and just add the word "zombie" in front of it. Your ship can be the *Zombie Carmichael* or the *Zombie Prince's Pride* and so forth.

In conclusion, your ship has to have a name, and you should select it from one of the above schools. Got the idea? Good. Now we still need to adorn your ship with one more thing . . .

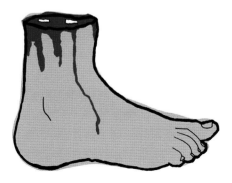

Zombie Pirate Flags

Why are pirate flags scary? Why do they send shivers up the otherwise stalwart spines of navies throughout the world?

It's not just the imagery. Skulls are scary, but not all pirate flags have skulls. Many have swords, hearts, devils, and other cool stuff. (Sure, these images might be more frightening than the Union Jack or something, but that bar is pretty low.)

Nope, what's scary about a pirate flag is **what it signifies.**

A considerable amount of information is transmitted through the flag a ship flies. First, there is the national alignment.

A ship's status as French or British or Spanish is signified by its colors. This is important, because it influences how the ships are likely to interact. If there is, say, a treaty between France and Spain, then a Spanish ship encountering the French flag would do well to avoid hostilities.

Beyond fealty to a certain nation, a ship's flag also signi-fies that a vessel has agreed to

> **ZOMBIE TIP:**
>
> **Keep your cutlass sharp but your eye-sight sharper.**
>
> Being able to notice the smallest speck on the horizon—be it a threat to you or a overloaded merchant ship bursting with valuable treasure and delicious humans—is an important skill for any zombie pirate captain. Keep your spyglass at the ready at all times!

"play by the rules." A ship flying colors agrees to adhere to the rules of maritime war and to the laws of that nation. Does Spain have rules against impressments? Does Great Britain grant quarter to captured hostiles? You can tell how a ship is going to fight based upon the allegiance of its flag.

Pirates have no allegiance to any nation, and they don't play by any rules. That might be the best way to understand the terror a pirate flag inspires.

Remember when you were a kid, and you'd be playing with your friends in the yard, and you'd all agree that you were superheroes or ninjas or secret agents protected by top-secret force fields? And remember how your big sister would come to get you for dinner, and she'd walk right up to you, and you'd protest, "You can't come close to me! I'm protected by a special high-tech force field!" And she'd respond: "I'm not playing." (Then she'd haul your butt inside.)

Anyhow, remember that? Because **that's** what pirate flags do.

A pirate flag says, "I'm not playing." All those rules and treaties you have? That whole "maritime law" thing your stuffy lawyers in wigs and smallclothes came up with? Those conventions about surrender and taking prisoners and sparing women and children?

Yeah, **we don't do that.**

A pirate flag says we're going to do whatever we want to do. A pirate flag says all those treaties on fancy parchment and all those medals on your chest don't matter to us. Your rank and rules will not protect you.

Pirate flags project the same warning as the guttural, undead moan of a zombie. Like pirates, zombies obey no treaties or rules. Those who fight zombies understand that they can expect no quarter from their enemy. There is no negotiation. Zombies accept no surrender and will never surrender themselves. Regal flags, gently worded entreaties, or impressive displays of armament will not dissuade a zombie from attacking. Zombies are gonna do what zombies are gonna do. Just like pirates.

As the captain of a zombie pirate ship, you can expect to instill the maximum horror possible in those who behold your colors (or, to be more precise, your color [hint: it will be black]). Not every pirate uses the traditional skull over crossed bones. You should feel encouraged to experiment with designs until you find something that feels like "you." Or maybe, "you with a shipload of flesh-hungry zombies."

Make your flag unique, but not too idiosyncratic. Let those who behold it understand that they are about to engage a pirate, but perhaps not *which* pirate. Just as a zombie creeps toward an unsuspecting victim for many long minutes before the victim suddenly realizes, "Hey, that's not just a drunk guy with a limp shuffling toward me. That's a zombie!" so it is to the advantage of a zombie pirate captain not to reveal the "zombie" element of the equation until it is too late for his opponent to take evasive maneuvers.

You want to make the zombie-centric elements of your flag subtle. If you must feature brains, shape them so that they may be mistaken as something else at a distance—say, cauliflower or a giant pink bean. Have fun with it. Consider a brain above crossed sabers, a yawning grave and crooked headstone, or even a simple zombie head with X's for eyes. Once they get close enough to appreciate the zombie design elements in your flag, your enemy will be too close to escape.

Remember: As a zombie pirate, your flag should say not only "We aren't playing by your rules," but also "We are going to eat you."

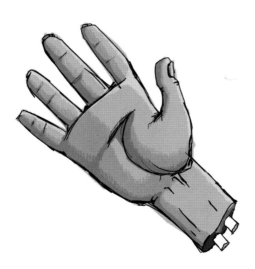

Your Zombie Pirate Uniform

To be a really effective zombie pirate, you need to make sure that your physical appearance commands respect from the zombies working under you and inspires terror in the nautical foes you face. The garb of a zombie pirate captain must serve a multitude of purposes. It is not altogether pirate, not altogether zombie. Striking the right balance is key.

The piratical aspects of your clothing will stem from practical concerns surrounding sea battles. You will wear heavy leather boots to protect your feet from splinters. (A deck can be easily turned into a field of splintered wood when directly targeted by enemy cannon fire.)

You will wear a thick leather belt (usually black or brown) cinched tightly at your waist. It must be heavy enough to serve as a makeshift holster for the many pistols it will hold. (You can augment your belt with leather straps that run diagonal across your chest, also for the purpose of holding pistols). Some pirates use scabbards for their cutlasses and daggers—which you may do, if you like—but the majority simply fasten these weapons to their belts as well.

If you have long or copious hair (looking in your direction, ladies), you will tie it back with a piece of string to keep it from getting in the way during battles. Unwieldy beards should also be secured with a string before combat begins. If you style yourself a sort of "gentleman zombie pirate" (which **can** be an effectively terrifying persona), you may wish to wear a powdered wig on your head. Further, keeping a shaved, wig-ready head aboard a pirate ship can reduce your exposure to lice and other creepy-crawlies that like to live on human hair. Keeping your own disgusting, tangled mane can make you look like a real wild man (or wild woman) and help you inspire terror in your enemies.

(Blackbeard famously takes this to the next level by lighting his hair and beard **on fire** during maritime engagements.)

If you have problems with sweat getting in your eyes, wearing a bandanna is also permissible. You may also wish to top it all off, literally, with a tricorne hat that provides protection from sunburn.

The above items of clothing—because they are functional—should always be kept in good working condition. You don't want holes in your boots allowing splinters and nails to go into your feet, and you don't want your belt or baldrics rotting away and your guns falling out. The above items need to be sound and functional at all times.

Other items in a zombie pirate captain's wardrobe could be—and *should* be—falling apart and rotting right off your body. (This will help signal your place among the undead.) These include your doublet or cloak, your breeches and pants, your waistcoat, your stockings, and your shirt. To be a proper zombie pirate, these items should be covered in dirt (preferably from a graveyard), filled with holes, and tattered in every way possible.

Are your clothes a few years out of style? Excellent. Only the most-recently reanimated zombies wear contemporary, trendy clothing. Try to pick out rotting coats and trousers that are at least fifty years old. This will help to establish you as a zombie pirate with old-school credibility who is above caring about the whims of fashion. Also, it will make you look like you've been dead and buried for a while, which is totally cool.

This inattention to your wardrobe's condition is essential for convincing the zombies around you that you're on the same team with them. (Probably, you have a bunch of voodoo charms and/or Satanic magic keeping the zombies in line, but appearances are important, too.) Zombie clothes impart an additionally terrifying aspect to your appearance. It lets your foes know that they're not just dealing with another pirate captain.

When humans witness a throng of zombies approaching them, several things stick out as "not right." The number of "not right" things increases as the zombies draw closer. (Those people in the distance are walking so slowly and stumbling around. It looks like now and then one of them will lose a shoe and not even notice it—not even stop to pick it up. Now that they're nearer, it looks like they're dirty, doesn't it? And some of their clothes seem to be old or ripped. And is that one naked?! And what's that red stuff dripping down from their mouths? Now I think they're moaning. Or are they maybe trying to say something? It sure sounds an awful lot like . . . "brains.")

As people approach you—be they fellow pirates, merchants about to get robbed and eaten, or just Caribbean locals—this "not-right-ness" should hit them as they get a good look at your clothing.

Finally, it should be noted that maintaining a zombie-like appearance has benefits during military engagements. When opposing military forces meet—be they European navy cruisers meeting at sea, or armies of 10,000 men fighting on land—it is **always** desirable to kill the commander(s) on the opposing side. In military lingo, this is often referred to as "decapitation." Kill the head and the body will die—or at least not know what to do. Less-qualified underlings will find themselves suddenly battlefield promoted and trying (badly) to run the show. Many militaries still haven't realized in the year 1700 that it's hard for an opposing military to kill your commanding officer **if they don't know which one he is.**

If you attack a European navy ship with your all-zombie crew, your opponents are probably going to notice you right away if you're the **only one** on your ship who doesn't look like a zombie. If, however, you dress yourself so as to fit in with the rest of your troops, you'll be safe from enemy sharpshooters (or, I mean, as sharp as shooters can be with muskets).

After a sea battle is over and you have emerged triumphant, you may wish to speak with the commanders of the vessel you have defeated (as you consider whether to rob, ransom, or throw them to the crowd of slavering zombies at your back). They will be wearing fancy caps and plumes and epaulets that mark them as the ones in charge. You will have no such demarcations, but it will be obvious to them that you are the zombie captain by the fact of your being able to speak (and that the zombies do not attack you). Unlike them, it is what you can **do** and not how you **appear** that makes you successful. The opposing commanders will realize only too late that their defeat probably has something to do with this.

A Zombie Pirate Nickname

Stereotypes. I hate 'em. You hate 'em. They're usually cruel and misinformed.

There are many negative stereotypes about pirates, but the worst (and most incorrect) is that they **always** have long, ornate nicknames (that can be generated using the formula of: Adjective, Given Name, Type of Precious Metal). Many pirates—in fact, let me be bolder, **most** pirates—do not have any sort of nickname at all.

Henry Morgan. Stede Bonnet. Anne Bonny. Francis Drake. Jean Fleury. François le Clerc. Edward Low. Mary Read. Charles Vane. These are **all** famous pirates of the Caribbean **who have never received a nickname.**

Zombies, however, often have nicknames. This is because nobody knows what else to call them.

Just try to think of all the famous zombies you know by name. There's "Fido." There's "Bub." There's "the Tarman Zombie." There's "That One Zombie That Impales the Girl's Eye on a Splinter."

That's about it. Not many zombies have proper names. Instead, they usually have descriptive nicknames recalling a notable physical feature of the zombie, or a notable act that the zombie has performed. You get names like: "That Zombie with a Tent Pole Sticking Through Him" and "That Zombie with No Legs" and "The Zombie That Ate My Sister-in-law."

With one or two exceptions, zombies are not given conventional names—you never hear of zombies called "Leroy Smith" or "Martha Jones"—because there is often a feeling that a zombie should be called something that **denotes its zombie-ness.** Giving zombies regular human names would be, in a very real sense, deceptive. After all, the rotting corpse lumbering toward you is **not** the person who used to inhabit that body, so calling a zombie who used to be Leroy Smith, "Leroy Smith" creates a dangerous confusion. Whatever you used to be named, if you're a zombie now, your old name's off the table. (The one exception to this rule is to insert the word "zombie" before the undead person's name, like "Mr." or "Dr." or something. For example, a zombie who used to be called Ty Cobb could now be called Zombie Ty Cobb.)

As the captain of a ship of zombie pirates, you straddle a very strange line between nicknaming conventions. Your involvement in the world of the undead suggests that you

> **ZOMBIE TIP**
> **Dead men tell no tales . . .**
>
> However, in the Caribbean of the 1700s, they **do** often come back as zombies—and usually, from the way they look (musket-ball holes, sword wounds, shark-teeth-shaped sections missing), you can hazard a pretty good guess about what happened to them . . . and find an appropriate nickname.

should have a nickname, and that it should be descriptive. However, you may also wish to incorporate elements of your piratical side. Focusing on accomplishments is a good place to start. If you sank a famous ship called the *Essex*, you could be known as Essex Sinker or maybe Essex Sinker Smith (or whatever your last name is). If you have a notable physical feature, you could lead with that. Hunchback Jones or Cross-eyes Miller are both perfectly acceptable. You should also feel comfortable putting "Zombie" or "Zombie Captain" in front of your name. (If Henry Morgan gets to be known as Captain Morgan, you can darn straight be Zombie Captain Fitzgerald or Zombie Captain Patel or whatever.)

As a zombie pirate captain, you have the opposite problem from that of someone like Blackbeard. Lots and lots of pirates have black beards. When Edward Teach chose to call himself "Blackbeard," thousands of pirates with black beards were like: "Damn, why didn't I think of that?" But importantly, having a nickname that draws attention to his black beard does not distinguish him on sight from all the similar pirates with dark facial hair. When a foolhardy soul comes aboard the *Queen Anne's Revenge* and seeks to address Blackbeard, he has to ask "Er . . . which one is he?" **You,** on the other hand, are the pirate captain of a ship of flesh-eating zombies. And, if you do it right, you'll be about the only one out there. While there are thousands of pirates with black beards, there should only be one marauding around in a ship filled with zombies. When folks see you pull into port in a shambling ship manned by the undead, there'll be no question as to who you are.

In conclusion, your zombie pedigree strongly suggests that you should pick a descriptive nickname. If you choose to keep your regular name, people will soon start mentally inserting " . . . the zombie pirate captain" after it, so there'll still be no question as to who you are.

Maximizing the Effectiveness of Your Zombie Crew

You've got your flag, your nickname, and your zombie pirate ship. You've also got a crew of brain-thirsty zombies ready to man your ship. You don't want to just let your zombies climb aboard all willy-nilly.

There's a right job for every zombie, and there are many jobs to be done aboard a pirate ship. Luckily, though, zombies bring a variety of advantages (and, yes, some disadvantages) to the table when it comes to running a ship.

Just as there are many types of zombies, so too are there many types of jobs aboard a zombie pirate ship. In addition to the captain (you), traditional pirate crews include a number of different jobs and positions. Some of these, however, become superfluous aboard a **zombie** pirate ship because of the unique character of the undead. These super-fluous positions include:

- **Master-at-Arms**—Aboard most ships, this person is the second in command to the captain, and charged with enforcing discipline and ensuring orders are carried out. As zombies get along with virtually all other zombies (only fighting in the rare instance when one mistakes another for a living human), having a disciplinarian aboard is not really necessary.

- **Quartermaster**—This person is traditionally charged with supplying necessities like food and rum to pirate crews. As zombie pirates require and desire only a steady diet of fresh brains, a Quartermaster's efforts to cook a tasty stew or distribute grog magnanimously would be completely bootless.

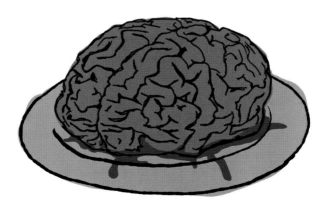

- **Ship's Doctor**—Yeah, not so much. Your crew is already dead, and the supply of zombies is fairly endless. I suppose you *could* keep somebody around to patch zombies up and sew their limbs back on when they get blasted apart by cannonballs, but in terms of cost-effectiveness, it's just not a great move. (If *you personally* are some kind of hypochondriac who wants a personal doctor aboard, then sure, go for it; but if you're not, then having one is largely unnecessary.)

Some traditional categories of sailor will stay the same on a zombie pirate ship and on a regular pirate ship, however, and you should ensure that you have some aboard. These include:

- **Boatswain (or "Bosun")**—Traditionally, this person is in charge of the decks, which is where things are loaded onto the ship—*things* like plundered treasure. (You see where I'm going with this.) I recommend making the biggest, strongest zombies in your crew boatswains. That way, after you capture an enemy ship, you can just tie a bunch of treasure to their backs and send your zombie boatswains toddling back over to your own ship. (Some zombie boatswains may still remember how to carry things, but fastening treasure to them with rope makes it a done deal.)

- **Carpenter**—Ideally, you want this specialized zombie to be the reanimated corpse of a deceased ship's carpenter (which is actually not all that hard to find in the Caribbean). While zombie pirate ships—like actual zombies—look a whole lot cooler when they're moldering and have a few missing parts, it's a problem when they become so seriously impaired that they can no longer move. You need to strike the right balance between "zombified and weird-looking" and "still able to chase after people." An undead ship's carpenter is just the zombie for the job. He will be able to ignore cosmetic damage to your ship's exterior (like chipped paint, rotting wood, or gaping cannonball holes), and thus be free to focus his time on important things like rudders, sails, and keeping the ship from sinking.

- **Gunner**—Though a zombie ship's carpenter is important, you likely want to save your highest-functioning zombies (the ones who retain the most humanlike qualities, and are able to be commanded and trained) for duty as gunners. Zombie pirates attack by making contact with an enemy ship and boarding it (or "infecting it") as quickly as possible. The goal, obviously, is never to sink or destroy an enemy vessel—except after you have looted its valuables and eaten its occupants. Yet the fact remains that cannons are essential to maritime warfare. You will want to fire on enemy ships to bring them into engagement with yours—and while sinking them on sight is undesirable, crippling or rendering them immobile is totally great. Employ your most capable zombies as gunners, and train them to aim for the masts, rudders, tillers, or large wooden steering wheels of enemy ships.

Finally, aboard a zombie pirate ship, there are some entirely original classifications of specialized sailors you need to select from your crew. These include:

- **Herder**—This zombie—who is preferably the reanimated corpse of a shepherd, crossing guard, or schoolmaster—has the important job of ensuring that members of your crew don't just walk overboard and fall into the sea. Certainly, your ship is going to have deck rails and safety ropes to keep the roamer-type zombies in your crew in line, but during rough seas or combat situations, there are going to be moments when a significant portion of your crew **just walking straight into the sea** becomes a real possibility. To help you with the onerous job of keeping your crew literally in line, employ these zombies with a natural herding instinct at any place where a boarding party nears the unprotected edge of a deck. (**Note:** The effectiveness of herders can sometimes be improved by attaching wooden planks or sections of fencing to them, essentially transforming them into walking rails or walls.)

- **Anchor**—While your ship is already full of actual metal anchors, you will also benefit from having two or three zombies who can serve topside as physical anchors during engagements. As you will recall, most zombies are bad at holding on to things and remaining still when humans are about. Anchors are zombies whose girth and stationary proclivities enable them to hold a position while other zombies are attacking (or to hold the end of a rope, if you put it underneath them). Usually, an anchor was an extremely overweight person in life. His or her legs—which could barely support such weight when they were, you know, not rotting away—have been weakened by decomposition and collapsed under the weight of the zombie. All that's left for you to do is to roll 'em into place.

- **Taster**—This specialized zombie is designed to flummox the crew of a besieged ship by pushing back its lines of defense. Tasters are so named because they advance from victim to victim after tasting just a small sample of a foe's brain. (Most zombies pause to consume a victim's **entire** brain before continuing on in search of more prey. In contrast, tasters need only a bite or two of brains before moving on to another victim.) Keeping tasters on the leading edge of any boarding party keeps your enemy moving backward as the tasters constantly advance in a search for more and more brains. Tasters will scatter enemy formations, and they also keep the deck of the ship from devolving into a giant picnic before the fighting is even through.

These highfalutin specializations aside, remember that the bulk of your crew is going to have the same title: **zombie pirate crewmember.** These are your go-to guys when things get exciting and the cannonballs start to fly. Though they are technically "unspecialized," they are still the heart and soul (and brains) of your crew. These are the zombies that will spill across ropes or planks or ladders and onto the decks of your enemy. They will fearlessly charge enemy guns, attacking with no concern for their own well-being. They will fight and fight and fight until they or their enemies are destroyed (and eaten). They will never surrender and never flee during combat.

So elevate certain zombies as you see fit for specialized tasks aboard your ship, but never forget that it's the "regular" members of your crew who will make your dreams of victory at sea a reality.

Preparations for the Hunt: Provisioning Your Ship and Readying Your Crew

Getting one's ship and crew ready to go to sea is an important and time-consuming part of any voyage. Merchants can spend weeks or even months loading a ship with goods, provisions for the crew, mail, weapons, and other assorted cargo. European navies ensure that their crews have been drilled for hundreds of hours on the tasks to be performed once onboard, both in and out of battle. Perhaps true to a stereotype, pirates are a bit more relaxed about things generally, but when it comes to making sure their ship is in good working order, you'd better believe they take it all very seriously. You would likewise do well to give your ship and crew the utmost attention before taking to the waters. Zombie pirates have special needs aboard a ship—specifically, you need there to be **a lot** of them—and other special things that they **don't** need. By packing in as many zombies as possible and bringing along only what you need, you'll help ensure a successful and profitable voyage.

Let's consider provisioning first. When you're dealing with zombie pirates, remembering to stock food aboard tends to be the least of your worries. Zombies do not "require" provisions like humans do. They can exist for long periods of time with no sustenance at all, and are not more effective crewmen if they are well fed. The only provision a zombie wants is brains. It wants live, thinking brains, torn freshly from a human skull. You're sailing out to sea with a crew of zombie pirates under the operative idea that it's the most expeditious way for them to get some brains (and for you to get rich in the bargain). As noted, there is **tremendous advantage** in the fact that you don't need to stock your ship's hold with food, water, rum, sleeping hammocks, or any of the other things that most ships carry. It also means that you are not required to purchase these things, which means more profit in the long run.

As they neither rest nor sleep, zombies have no need to recline once aboard. (Zombies aren't particular about personal space either, so feel free to pack 'em in real tight if you like. Many a zombie pirate's hold looks like a seething mass of flesh and bones, but on closer inspection is revealed to be a collection of very tightly packed zombies.)

A more interesting task presents itself in the form of fitting your zombies for a tour at sea and administering appropriate training. If you've done things right, many (or even most) of the zombies in your retinue will be the reanimated corpses of dead pirates. Thus, they will come equipped with cutlasses clutched in their bony fingers,

> **ZOMBIE TIP**
>
> **Limit your friends and associates**
>
> You didn't get into this line of work because you're a "people person." Really, you're more of an "eating people person." Plus, fewer living humans around means more treasure for you, doesn't it?

wooden legs installed as needed, and menacing hooks screwed into empty sockets where hands used to be. Though most zombies attack using only their hands and teeth, it is still possible for higher-functioning zombies to remember how to use a sword or pistol in combat. Don't get too frustrated if some of your pirate zombies end up having a sword that is "just for show" and neglect their cutlasses in favor of biting and scratching when it's time for a fight. This is to be expected. (The horde that storms across your deck and onto your enemy's doesn't need to be trained in elegant swordplay. There just have to be a lot of them. Zombies win by overwhelming force of numbers.)

Anything you can do to make your zombies appear more terrifying is always welcome. As your victories at sea begin to mount, this will occur naturally. Few things are more terrifying than seeing something that was once a symbol of safety and protection turned into something that wants to kill you (and eat your brain). As you "harvest" new zombie crew members from navies and merchant ships that you defeat, your crew will begin to become populated with zombie pirates who are still wearing the uniforms of the British or French or Spanish navies. This will have a supremely devastating effect upon those who encounter you, as they struggle to reconcile the "friendly" British navy men who are now ripping flesh with their teeth and gibbering to eat people alive.

When it comes to actually *training* the zombies, there will be very little to do. The previous chapter has already dealt with the particular classes of zombies who can be extracted from the rest of the horde and given specialized tasks. Once this much is done, the trick is simply getting the remainder of the unskilled zombies on your ship. Because you are their captain and creator (and likely bound to them by a number of netherworldly charms), your zombie pirate crew members will never attack you, no matter how forcefully you ram them twenty-deep into your hold using the ass-end of an oar. What I'm saying here is go ahead and be forceful with your zombie pirates. You should not only fill your deck with zombies but also pack them so tightly into the ship that they can explode out as if spring-loaded and overwhelm your foes.

As a zombie pirate captain, your role is more about harnessing the forces inherently in play within zombies than teaching them something they don't already know. A zombie's atavistic need to consume flesh will make it do certain things when edible humans are near. Your job in loading and preparing your ship is simply to position the zombies so that these inevitable reactions work to your advantage.

When it finally takes to the seas, your zombie pirate ship should be creakingly heavy and **completely full of zombies.** This is how a zombie pirate captain defines "battle ready."

How "Slow" Now Equals "Absolutely Terrifying"

Moving slowly. Preying upon things. Sound like anybody you know? Of course it does. It sounds like zombies.

Zombies are natural pirates because they are already attuned to a "life" of roaming and attacking. They take what they need (brains), and leave what they don't need (everything else). Zombies also understand—or *seem* to understand—that remaining stationary means destruction.

Zombies, like pirates, aren't hard to kill on a one-on-one basis. They die with a simple decapitation or musket ball to the head. They tend to move slowly. (Pirates may have peg legs, but zombies have crushing rigor mortis and tendons that have often rotted away entirely. While pirates are often drunk and/or delusional, zombies comport themselves with the kind of massive loss of function that only comes with years spent moldering in a graveyard.) If you want to catch up with a single roaming zombie, it's not going to be hard to put him down provided you have even the most basic of weapons. A *stationary* zombie is completely a lost cause. (A stationary zombie is also not going to get to eat anybody's brain.) That's why every zombie—no matter how desiccated and bony, no matter how many limbs or appendages it may be missing—always drags itself along and is always in a group. Movement and comradeship mean survival and the possibility of delicious brains. Inactivity and isolation mean destruction and no brains.

While a single roaming zombie may seem like a threat to very few—and may, in fact, seem quite comical and amusing—a horde of zombies (or a pirate ship bursting at the seams with them) is a terrifying sight to behold. Zombies and pirates move slowly, but as long as they move (and as long as there are a lot of them) they are still a threat.

When a stuffy British navy lookout cries "Pirates off the starboard bow!" it may still be a full hour from this first sighting until these piratical aggressors have moved close enough to put their cannons in range.

Yet, the fact that it will, you know, **be awhile** before the pirates get here does nothing to diminish the alarm and anxiety that the British sailors suddenly feel. Same thing with a zombie outbreak. When the first few walking corpses shamble into the fledgling settlement that will one day become Port-au-Prince, the villagers can easily evade and avoid these slow-moving visitors. However, the abject terror they feel will come not from these two or three brain-seeking interlopers, but from their knowledge that the main burying ground just outside town holds *hundreds* of corpses—who at this very moment may be clawing their way out of the earth and heading toward the smell of living humans.

In both cases, slow is scary. In both cases, the fact that any real physical danger is like an hour away does **nothing** to quell the concerns of those who will be preyed upon.

As a zombie pirate captain, you're going to be doubly slow. Your boat is slow and your pirates are slow. The good news is that you're also going to be doubly terrifying to your enemies (and just doubly awesome, generally). When a trading ship laden with spoils from the New World sights your rotting zombie bark off the starboard bow, the captain will understand that your ship is a massive pirate barge (slow) and—when he looks more closely—that your crew is composed entirely of lumbering, loping zombies (slower). Your lack of speed, however, will cease to occupy the unlucky merchant's mind to the same degree as your lack of compunction about eating him and everyone else aboard. He will also, as he thinks about it, become creepingly aware of the terrifying advantages that **zombie** pirates will bring to bear against him.

Though their ship might move slowly through the water, the zombies steering it will never tire or rest. They will never need to sleep. They will never run out of provisions. While a merchant's crew is prey to every human weakness and failing, your **inhuman** zombie pirate crew can work around the clock to chase the merchant to some craggy shoal where he will have to choose between fleeing overboard or putting up a (bootless) armed resistance. As much as he may hate you, he will not have time to scuttle his craft.

As you internalize the Code of Zombie Piracy, embrace your inner slowness. Understand that it works for you, and not against you. Zombie pirate crews—much like hordes of terrestrial zombies on foot—always get their man.

Eventually.

Yo, Ho, Ho, and
Now Let's Eat Some People
(a.k.a. "Prey")

Keeping a zombie crew happy means one thing and one thing alone: brains. To begin your career of marine predation, you will need to strike where you can plunder treasure and your crew can plunder cranial tissue. What magical, wonderful place makes both of these things concurrently possible? The answer is *trade routes*.

The great nations of Europe have a constant stream of ships going to and from the New World. Most of these streams run through the Caribbean at some point. (The whole reason the Europeans got focused and mean was that they realized there was money to be made.) Finding these merchant routes is not a difficult project. (Their locations are not exactly a secret.) Using them to hunt isn't difficult either—as long as you follow the rules of this Code.

Some things are safe from pirates. Some things—even things of great value—pirates **do not want.** Vast Caribbean sugar plantations? Pirates have no use for them. Sure, they might sack a plantation and take all the women and rum, but they're not going to stick around and occupy it. Trading ports? No more than a passing interest. Pirates might look for a friendly port in which to dock and provision, but they aren't there to set up shop. Colonial forts and military installations? Not so much. Unless there is a personal grudge between the pirates and the soldiers inside, these two shall never meet.

Remember, as you begin your career of trade route predation, that it is **all about movement.** You must be a thing that moves, and so must your prey. Pirates who don't move starve. Pirates who don't move get hunted down off the coast of North Carolina by the British Navy and killed. Pirates who don't move are just a bunch

ZOMBIE TIP

It is, it is a glorious thing. . .

To watch a crew of zombies feasting on the brains of your enemies, to see enlisted navy crews wetting themselves in abject fear when your flag is raised, and to help yourself to the kind of spoils that can only be obtained through large-scale nautical murder. If you want to sing a silly song about it, too, I guess that'd be all right.

of stinky bored guys on a ship with no money. For pirates, movement is life. Movement provides new prey each and every day and also helps keep the exact location of the pirates a mystery (so they do not become prey themselves).

Pirates are adopters and adapters. They are the hermit crabs of the seas and coastlines. (Actually, hermit crabs are the hermit crabs of the seas and coastlines, but try and follow me here. . . .) When pirates capture a ship that's bigger and better than theirs, they are liable to adopt it as their new home and scuttle the old one. When they find a cache of sharper cutlasses and better pistols, they take them and throw their own rusty swords away. Pirates harbor no sentimental attachment to possessions.

Like zombies, pirates must prey upon every appropriate person. Like zombies, pirates do not discriminate when it comes to whom they attack.

If you're new to the maritime world, you might have the idea that the merchant vessels that sail along trade routes from Europe to the Caribbean are slow and unarmed. This could not be further from the truth. Any ship carrying something across the Atlantic is going to be ready for a fight—with pirates, yes, but also with unfriendly navies (or natives). Merchant ships have to be ready for anything. Merchant ships carry cannons, guns, and crews that are ready to use them. They also carry riches worth plundering. Make no mistake, as a pirate (or zombie pirate) your main focus is merchant ships (even if they are hard nuts to crack).

Depending on how laden they are with cargo—which is largely worthless to you (you want money and valuables, not 2,000 pounds of wool)—these merchant vessels will display varying rates of speed. You are piloting a zombie ship that, like a zombie itself, will be slow and falling apart in many places. Based on this, you want to avoid things that make other ships want to split. This is easier said than done, because one of the things that makes Caribbean merchant ships sail as hastily as possible in the opposite direction is **the presence of other ships.**

If you look at it, this reaction to another sail on the distant horizon does make a kind of sense. Unless the merchant captain is in distress and needs assistance, there is almost nothing good that can come of inter-action with another ship. In the worst case, the ship in the distance can turn out to be pirates, yes—but it can also turn out to be the navy of a nation at war with the merchant's nation. This opposing navy might sink the merchant ship or seize its cargo as war spoils. Even a navy ship from the merchant's *own country* is not entirely welcome, as it would be within its powers to stop the merchant and inspect his ship for contraband, evidence of smuggling, unpaid taxes, and so forth.

Merchant ship captains want not to be bothered. Their ideal voyage is a completely uneventful one. (I know . . . boring, right?)

So when you spot a merchant ship that looks ripe for the taking, your first—and, indeed, most difficult—step is not to scare it off. You should begin by charting a course that bisects the route of the merchant, but is not necessarily the shortest path from your boat to his. Make it appear—if possible—that your ships' coming near to one another is a coincidence of your respective routes.

Next, as soon as you can ascertain the merchant's country of origin, you should fly a flag of that nation. (Have an extensive flag menu onboard to choose from, even flags from landlocked countries that don't have navies. You never know, right?) It is optimal to appear from a distance to be a friendly fellow merchant.

What induces merchants to meet? The captain of the vessel you've targeted may wish to stop and trade with you or exchange information about the price of goods in different ports. The key is getting the merchant comfortable with sailing a course in which your ships will intersect (or at least draw near), for once this is set into motion it will be exceedingly difficult to suddenly reverse.

When the merchant ship (hereafter called "prey") draws near, you should appear on deck dressed as a merchant yourself. (The most tasteless and gaudy clothing you have captured should be set aside for this purpose. Add an artificial paunch constructed with a belt and some pillows, and boom, you're transformed into a gouty old millionaire.) Hail the fellow merchant—possibly by waving an embroidered handkerchief—and indicate that you have something to communicate. You can also entice them by holding up a valuable or rare commodity.

If you succeed in this ruse, and the fool draws near, have your crew members attach your two ships with grappling hooks and lay down boarding planks. By the time that the merchant realizes that your crew members are **bloodthirsty zombies,** it will be too late, and the two ships will already be attached. You can now open your ship's hold and allow your zombie minions to flood over his decks like a wave. All human matter will be consumed. Soon the deck will be littered with things that zombies don't care about, like gold and valuables. After this is accomplished, you can sack the merchant ship personally, and at your leisure.

If, however, your initial charade is not successful, and the merchant hesitates to parley with you (or even fires on you), you should treat the engagement as though you were attacking not a merchant, but a naval vessel. The rules for this are covered subsequently.

Battles, Broadsides, and Brains (or How to Fight European Navies)

Sometimes you will not be preying upon merchant ships, but will instead be required to face a fully armed European navy war vessel. The prospect may be more daunting and less fun than picking off sea traders by means of a ruse. Still, there's no reason a competent zombie pirate captain can't expect a consistently optimal outcome when fighting navy ships, too.

Most nautical battles are slow, awkward affairs. Zombies are well suited to this because of their natural affinity for doing things at a leisurely pace. If you fancy yourself a zombie pirate captain (or a sea captain of any stripe), you had better make like a zombie and become infinitely unhurried and patient.

Do you have somewhere to be today? A few errands you'd like to run later? A date with a comely lass tonight on Hispaniola? If you do, you better not start a sea battle, because these things can take *all fucking day.* Six hours. Seven hours. Even eight is not unheard of. That's **after the fighting has started.** That doesn't include the hours and hours of hunting one another and slowly bringing one another into range. Every part of sea combat is slow.

After hours and hours of hunting one another, the two ships will finally engage one another like giant, lumbering animals. Orders are barked intensely and sailors scurry about frantically on the decks, but the ships themselves creak and teeter around with what can only be described as maddening, frustrating slowness. Even when the battle is joined in earnest, there are usually codified (and slow) stages by which the combat progresses.

In the opening of the encounter, the parties involved will attempt to position themselves for optimal use of their respective ships' advantages. Ships are typically armed with cannons mounted on little beds with wheels. These cannons are the most powerful weapons aboard, and ships usually choose to engage one another only if their cannons appear to be at least equal to those of their enemy. Some ships will also carry smaller hand cannons called "swivel guns" mounted along the rails. (These weaker but more precise cannons can be used against an enemy ship or against an enemy boarding party.) Because firing cannons and swivel guns creates a lot of smoke, much of the slow, awkward jockeying before the fight will be an attempt to engage upwind from the enemy. That way, the smoke from the cannons—and later from the muskets and pistols—will blow into the faces of the enemy's gunners.

When the ships finally draw within range, the big cannons start firing. Where the cannons are aimed is usually determined by the goal of each ship's captain. If the goal is to terminally cripple, sink, or destroy a ship, the cannons will be aimed at the body of that ship. If a captain's goal is to take the other ship more or less intact (or to induce it to disengage, surrender, or flee), that ship's cannons will be aimed at the enemy's decks for the purpose of killing as many of its crew as possible. (Killing the enemy captain himself is ideal.)

The kind of shot put into the cannons will also be determined by the desired fate of the opposing ship. A captain seeking to destroy the ship he faces will use the classic cannonballs we all know and love. However, a captain seeking chiefly to kill the enemy crew will be more likely to use variations on the traditional cannonball; things with names like grapeshot, chain shot, and bar shot. Unlike a cannonball, which tends to punch a relatively small hole in the hull of a ship, these "shot-based" missiles spin or spray wildly and can create a hail of deadly shrapnel that goes flying across a ship's deck.

Okay, so remember how the ships hunted one another slowly and engaged each other kinda slowly? Once the shooting starts, things still go kind of slowly. A ship's cannons are doing well if each one gets off a shot every **eight minutes** or so. (That's if things are going *well.* Ships with cannon crews that suck might only get off three or four shots per cannon for *every hour* of fighting.) Yet despite the slow pace of things, there are still ways that a nautical battle can end at this stage, usually via surrender. Ships can suffer so many cannon breaches to the hull that they actually start sinking. Ships can catch on fire, and the fire can rage out of control. Most dramatically of all, ships can explode. (In the 1700s, the term "powder room" is not a euphemism for where women go to the bathroom. Rather, it refers to an actual room aboard a ship where gunpowder is stored. If this room sustains a direct hit—perhaps early in a battle, when its reserves are still very full—the entire ship can be blown apart like a giant floating grenade.)

However, if a ship has not been sunk, set afire, or exploded completely, the attacking captain may wish to board it. This is accomplished optimally by pulling alongside. (This is called "boarding midships.") The attacking crew will use all manner of ropes, hooks, chains, and medieval pikes to secure one ship to the other. While portrayals abound of pirates swinging from ship to ship on ropes, the vastly more expedient practice involves simply putting down a plank and running across it. (Believe it or not, pirate ships do not have planks just to make people walk them.) Alternately, the ships can be pulled so close that they are actually touching, thereby eliminating the need for ropes or planks entirely.

Those boarding can expect to be met with fierce resistance (or not, depending on how well their cannons have eliminated the opposing crew members). At this point, the cannon fire ceases altogether as entirely new weapons are brought to bear. Muskets and pistols will feature prominently. Swivel guns will be fired at close range. This initial gunpowder-based exchange will be deadly. It will also be over quickly. Once people start jumping from deck to deck and rushing at one another, it's going to be hard to stop and reload anything. Thus, you can expect an initial exchange of gunfire, followed by hand-to-hand combat. (Higher-ranking and wealthier crew members—and ranking military officers—are likely to have more than one pistol. Some will carry ten or fifteen. The thing about pistols, though, is that once they're shot, they're shot. You'd be surprised how fast you can go through fifteen pistols when there are a bunch of guys trying to kill you. Because of this, even a zombie pirate captain packing serious heat would also do well to practice his swordplay.)

A pirate sword is called a "cutlass." (Nobody knows why, but it is convenient that a brawny female pirate carrying one may thus fairly be called "a cut lass with a cutlass.") Curved blades and S-shaped cross-guards typically distinguish cutlasses. The hilts of cutlasses are often fancy and ornate, especially if the owner is wealthy. As swords go, cutlasses tend to be on the shorter side. (If a pirate carries a second blade in addition to his cutlass, it will be something even shorter, like a short sword or dagger.) Cutlasses are as long as swords get in naval warfare. Pirates never carry long swords or fencing rapiers, and for good reason. When the fighting begins, it will be everywhere. In most cases, it will spread to every part of the deck of both ships. **It will be very crowded, and it will be hard to maneuver.** Luckily, cutlasses are not made for the dramatic, sweeping strokes and feints one can essay on an open field. There isn't room for such fancy-lad sword fighting on a ship's crowded deck. Cutlasses are made for short-range stabbing and hacking because **that will be the only kind of swordplay going on.**

In addition to swords and pistols, you can also expect to encounter a "potpourri" category of weapon. These should not be forgotten or ignored, for they can prove just as deadly as any blade or lead ball. For example, when two battling ships physically touch one another, combatants often use long poles with hooks or blades to pull the ships closer to one another. These poles can also be used to repel boarders, or can be thrown like spears. You can also expect improvised grenades, flaming bottles of high-proof rum, and all manner of heavy pointed things to come flying across at you. (If something is throwable, expect it to be thrown!) In melees that are not settled quickly—and in which powder is exhausted, bayonets are bent, and swords are blunted—expect anything with a handle to be used as a weapon. Axes meant for chopping rope will be used for chopping heads. Pots and pans from the scullery will be used to strike people in the face. Metal and wood debris can often be found in the right shape and size to make it an improvised weapon.

Hand-to-hand fighting on deck is the final stage of most nautical confrontations. It can end when one side is completely eradicated, but more frequently ceases when the losing ship realizes the cause is lost and surrenders. If the winning side is a European navy or merchant, then the defeated crew will likely be executed or thrown into the brig (where they will be transported back to a European nation, be tried for piracy [or for being in the navy of a different European nation], found guilty, and executed). If the winning side is a bunch of pirates, it's a bit more complicated. The defeated crew may be:

- Executed
- Marooned
- Held for ransom
- Invited to become pirates themselves

The pirates will also plunder the captured ship, and may even take the ship itself (if it's still intact enough to be useful). Being subject to no laws governing their comportment, the whim of the conquering pirate captain can dictate the fate of the captured opponents.

Now . . .

Zombie pirates will fight differently than regular pirates (or navies or merchant crews). However, as an enterprising zombie pirate captain, it's important that you understand the typical nautical warfare paradigm into which you will be entering. It's important that you understand it, because you are going to **destroy and upend it utterly.**

As captain of a ship of zombie pirates, you will also engage your prey through a series of stages that will be vastly different than those governing most naval warfare.

Like a zombie, you will stalk your opponents. You will approach them slowly. Like a moldering corpse, your rotting pirate ship will not appear much of a threat. You will show persistence and continue to pursue your prey, even as it moves to avoid you (not so much out of fear as from a sense of "ick, gross"). Stay on him, and the opposing captain will eventually think to himself: "These guys just won't go away. Well, if a fight is really what they **want** . . ."

Make the enemy captain feel bad about it . . . like attacking you involves being unnecessarily cruel. (He will realize only too late that it was you who had the upper hand all along, and that it is *he* who is to become the recipient of cruelty.) When the ship you are pursuing comes into range for cannon fire, you can expect to be subjected to at least one volley. If, as is likely, your opponent feels that his ship obviously outmatches yours, he may simply fire a warning shot to show he is serious. (You may fire back if you like, but it is not compulsory.)

Your goal in nautical combat—like a zombie's in terrestrial combat—is to **come into physical contact with the enemy as soon as possible.** As long as your enemy keeps his ship separate from yours—and can fire at you—he holds an advantage. However, the moment your ships touch one another, **you own him.**

You must pull alongside your enemy and latch your grappling hooks into his deck as quickly as possible. If you must fire your cannons, load them with balls connected to long chains that can physically link your ship to whatever you shoot at.

"But what of repeated cannonades and broadsides?" you might be tempted to ask at this point. "They're so dramatic and cool-looking. If we're only going to make the initial volley our priority, why do we even have cannons at all? They sure weigh a lot, and our ship could probably go much faster if we didn't have them."

Here's the thing, smart guy. Cannons are valuable for their ability to cripple opposing ships, even in an opening volley. (Zombies are experts at picking on the immobile and crippled.) Moreover, the presence of cannons makes it appear to the enemy that you intend to engage them using the typical tactics of nautical warfare. This subterfuge gives you an important advantage. If your ship visibly lacked cannons entirely, and yet you steered right for a heavily armed enemy, even the greenest captain would understand that something was "up."

The great thing about engaging an enemy at sea is that it's really, really hard to disengage. (It's great for **you,** actually, and not so much for whomever you're fighting.) Once your enemy decides to let you get close enough that he can fire on you, he has made an irreversible commitment. Barring a sudden change in wind direction, there is no way for your enemy to back away quickly. That, ironically, is exactly what he is going to want to do when he notices that those slavering pirates on your decks look like slavering zombies the closer he drifts. When you hit him with the grappling hooks and ropes, all doubt will vanish from his mind. He is facing a crew of zombie pirates, and he just let them get close enough to strike.

Once you have made this physical connection between ships, your next goal is getting as many zombies as possible up on the decks and in the fight. (Again, zombies lose in situations where there are just a few of them and humans have room to maneuver. Zombies win in situations where they outnumber humans who have nowhere to flee.) Once you get the planks and rope ladders in place, your zombie pirate crew will do the rest. Zombies are innately attracted to humans, and will always find the shortest possible distances between themselves and people they want to eat.

That said, don't send your favorite zombies in first. Zombie boarding parties move slowly, and are notoriously easy targets. Your opponents will have loaded pistols and dry powder. At least for a while.

Though the first few waves of your zombies may go down with relative ease, the horde that spills out from your deck will show no signs of slowing. (I mean, yes, their advance will already be pretty slow to start with, but you get the idea.) Your zombie pirates will advance with no sense of self-preservation. They have no "long-term plans" for themselves (get a little treasure, find a nice girl, retire to a tropical island somewhere . . .). No. Your zombie pirates just go straight for brains, whether or not they're behind a line of loaded muskets.

Once your enemy has exhausted his powder, then the real fun will begin. As your hold begins to empty—revealing more and more zombies, because, hey, you don't need to carry around provisions and rum—your foes will find themselves fighting an enemy that greatly outnumbers them. They will also find themselves in an enclosed space with nowhere to go except the sea. They will curse the fact that their cutlasses are designed for stabbing and hacking (and not clean, long blades, facilitating decapitation) and that they are curved at the end (making stabbing through a zombie's skull and into its brain all the more difficult).

As the enemy crew members begin to go down, many attacking zombies will cease fighting and instead sit down to eat their defeated foes. This is no cause for concern. For every zombie who stops to munch, two zombies behind it will step up to take its place.

As the battle wanes and the opposing crew begins to sense its inevitable defeat, a few craven sailors may elect to throw themselves overboard. Presumably, being eaten by sharks is better than being eaten by zombies. (Sharks have bigger mouths, so maybe it takes less time?) It is important that your zombie pirates **do not pursue these fleeing humans overboard.** Many a zombie pirate captain has lost a significant portion of his or her crew when a group of tasty sailors all made a break for it at the same time.

To prevent this loss, I recommend corralling the final group of surviving humans **away** from the rails of the ship. This is easier than you might think, but you've got to give them somewhere to go. (Just as zombies will always move toward humans, humans will always move away from zombies whenever there is space to do so.) I recommend allowing the final holdout group of survivors to "escape" belowdecks where you can deal with them later. You can also corral them toward any ropes or rope ladders that might allow them to climb up into the rigging (or even up to the crow's nest). They'll have evaded you in the short term, but will have nowhere to go and no hope of escape. (Somewhere in your crew there have got to be some zombies with all their limbs that can still climb ladders.)

By forsaking a battle of cannons in favor of closing in to make physical contact with another ship, you can reliably defeat any foe in the navies of Europe. Your unconventional fighting style and the undead status of your crew will combine to create an unstoppable force. (What you do with the plundered armaments and captured treasure is up to you.) Keep in mind that beyond merchants and navies, there are other foes yet to consider. . . .

Facing Off Against Other Pirates

I hope it's been made adequately clear by this point that you are in the Caribbean to attack merchants to enrich yourself and to attack European navies because they suck and are mean bullies. Other pirates are not meant to be a regular item on your menu. It is better that a collegial brotherhood (or sisterhood, as the case may be) should exist between rival pirate crews. Friendly competition (to be the first to plunder a ship or discover hidden treasure) should be the extent of your "conflict."

Now and then, personal vendettas and local politics will conspire such that you will find yourself facing off against another pirate crew in a fight. When this occurs, it is always

the duty of the captains—much like seconds in a duel—to see what can be done to avoid armed conflict.

As the captain of a zombie pirate ship, you face little danger from conventional pirates. Your undead horde can defeat virtually any human crew. However, there is always time and expense involved. There is the potential for your ship to be damaged and for some zombies to be lost. If the pirate crew you are facing is a group of relative neophytes, they may have very little treasure worth appropriating after the battle is through. Fighting them is long on investment and short on reward. For these and other reasons, I advise raising a white flag and attempting to negotiate with the opposing pirate captain before cannonballs start to fly.

When a violent encounter with another pirate ship is unwanted, the following attempts at a peaceful resolution are recommended:

Propose your differences be settled through gambling— Most pirates are stone-cold gambling addicts, and pirate captains are no exception. (Ship-to-ship warfare may, itself, be considered the ultimate gamble by some [especially when neither ship is staffed with the undead]). Because it is so rife, some pirate crews have tried to adopt rules against gambling—they'll write them right in the ship's charter—but these are rarely followed. It's not uncommon for unlucky pirates to return to port with nothing to show for a series of successful conquests because they've gambled away their shares while still onboard. Despite shipboard prohibitions against it that he may have signed (or, indeed, drawn up himself), the opposing pirate captain is almost certainly dying to have a gambling relapse. In some cases, you can provide this relapse while averting conflict at the same time. Propose to the captain that you settle your differences with a game of pitch-and-toss, dice, or three-card monte. The loser shall forfeit his ship and treasure to the winner (and whatever else it takes to get this guy interested). If the opposing pirate captain agrees, then count yourself lucky: No matter what happens, you win. If you beat the pirate captain at the gambling game of his selection, then you defeat him bloodlessly. If you "lose" your ship to him in the course of the wager, you have to merely refuse to honor the agreement and fight him for it anyway. (This is called "being a cheater and liar." It is part of being a pirate, in case you weren't clear on that.)

Invite the opposing pirate captain (and his crew) to become zombies—This might seem counterintuitive, but bear with me here. If you can open a parley at all with this guy who wants to fight you, you'll probably learn that he is relatively new to piracy and/or the Caribbean. (He wants to attack a ship full of zombies, after all. How seasoned could he be?) You don't need to be a skilled orator to make a convincing case that—if they stop and think about it—the captain and his crew might enjoy themselves a whole lot more as members of the walking dead. Invite them to consider the awesome ability of being able to take a cutlass through the torso or a bullet to the heart without so much as momentary discomfort. Ask them to imagine how cool it will be to never get old and "die" (in the traditional sense). Ask them if they've even been curious about what the brains of their enemies might taste like. You're bound to have at least a few takers, even if the captain himself remains unconvinced. Welcome any undead recruits aboard your ship and see that they are bitten (not eaten) so that zombification can begin. Even if you must fight the opposing pirate captain, you will find that his crew is now at least somewhat diminished, and your own expanded.

Settle things with a duel—Pirates—all pirates—love to duel. Duels settle things publicly. Duels have a clear winner and loser. Duels are a way to assert bravery and skill and to show off for women. And here, really, is the important thing to remember about them: *The winner of the duel is the one who is not dead.* You'll notice, here, that I don't say "The winner of the duel is the one who fights honorably," or "The winner of the duel is the one who refrains from using flash powder, blinding mirrors, or other tools of misdirection," or even "The winner of the duel is the one who doesn't pull out a pistol and shoot the other guy as he's drawing his sword, and then say, 'Oh, wait . . . Did you mean we were doing a sword-fighting kind of duel? Oh my. Where *is* my head today . . . ?'" Whatever manner of subterfuge and trickery you might wish to employ is fine, as long as it leaves your enemy dead and you alive. If there is *any chance* that the duel will be a fair fight, you shouldn't do it. Putting your own life in danger makes no sense when you've got a ship filled with bloodthirsty zombie pirates waiting for the word to settle things for you. To be clear: Duels offer the advantage of expediency, but are a lousy choice if you're going to "fight fair" and "actually risk your life."

If these invitations do not tempt the opposing pirate captain, you may find yourself back where you started and should prepare yourself to fight an opposing ship of pirates. To fight your enemy effectively, you must understand him. Luckily for you, you are also a pirate.

The main difference between pirates and European navy ships—the two entities most likely to intentionally attack you—is the *motivation* behind their attacks. Navies attack you because it is their job. The navy captain may be seeking fame and glory as "the vanquisher of the dreaded zombie pirates," but the enlisted men aboard his ship are just putting in a day's work. They do not draw additional pay if you are defeated, and will receive no portion of your captured loot.

Pirate crews, very much to the contrary, are there for personal gain. Each pirate opposing you—from the captain to the cook—is thinking about the share of the treasure he's going to get. If the pirates have been chasing you for a while, they may be low on

ZOMBIE TIP

There is no "I" in team . . .

There is, however, an "I" in pirate. It's the second letter. Also, it's representative of how pirates are all out for themselves.

supplies. Attacking you may be their best hope for replenishing themselves.

Their every reason for attacking you is revealed as **profoundly misguided** on close examination. There is likely some treasure aboard, yes, but most of your hold has been filled with zombie pirates. Aside from a personal stash in your cabin, the rest of your loot has been buried or hidden, and is not aboard. Also, with a crew that does not eat or drink, there is going to be very little in the way of food and water for opposing pirates to capture. And—I don't care how much of a lush you are—your personal rum supply is **not** going to go very far in slaking the thirst of an entire pirate crew. The best strategy for defeating an opposing crew of pirates is to make the above facts clear to them in a way that will demoralize them just at the moment they begin to attack you.

As with any zombie-against-pirate sea battle, the first step is to get in close and connect your ship to theirs with the aid of grappling hooks. You make take a few cannonballs amidships early on, but this is expected with any engagement. When contact is made, and grappling hooks have secured the two ships together, proceed to **open every window, hatch, gun port, and door onboard.** You want the attacking pirates—at this crucial moment, as they ready their pistols, unsheathe their swords, and prepare to make the leap onto your decks—to see very clearly that the inside of your zombie pirate ship **only contains more zombies.** The main hatch on your deck should erupt open like a giant grave overflowing with the undead. Pirates on the upper levels of the opposing ship who look down into it should be able to see firsthand that the hold of your ship contains nothing except more zombies.

Here, there is room to let mystery and fear of the supernatural take over as well. (You are, after all, the captain of a ship of zombies.) Let the pirates who oppose you begin to wonder about exactly what kind of foe they are facing. Maybe the zombies in your hold go on forever. Maybe your ship is a portal to hell or another dimension where zombies live. Maybe these zombies are restless, ceaseless fighters who will stop at nothing until the brains of their foes have been eaten. (They'll be right about that last one, at least.)

While opening every part of the ship does make you more vulnerable to certain kinds of attack, the corresponding effect on your enemies makes this a risk worth taking. In most cases, your opponents will be too paralyzed with fear to act. Also, they will start wondering if there's anything aboard your ship other than zombies. With any luck, dissent will begin to spread through the ranks of the opposing pirates as they remind one another that, hey, we signed up for this to make ourselves rich, not because we like killing zombies.

Fighting a crew of the undead was probably a shaky proposition in the first place. If you can make it appear that their captain now wishes them to fight an enormous crew of zombie pirates **for no discernable financial reward,** you may inspire a full-scale mutiny. (A proper, organized mutiny will not be possible during a battle, but you may see the opposing pirates locking their captain in the brig, trying frantically to disengage their ship from yours, or just jumping overboard and swimming away.) Then, when the opposing pirates are degenerating into total disarray, **you** can take **their** ship.

In conclusion, it's always disappointing when you're put in a position where you have to attack a fellow brother of the skull-and-crossbones fraternity, but it's better to be prepared than to leave these things up to chance. Because they are highly motivated outlaws, you would put yourself into peril by underestimating them. Yet by challenging their captain directly and making clear that you have little of value aboard (other than hungry zombies), you can virtually guarantee a positive outcome.

Replenishing Your Crew at Sea: Out with the Old, In with the Undead

Let's face it . . . As totally awesome as zombies are, after enough time has passed, some of them can cease to be useful.

Years on the high seas can wear zombies out. They can be reduced to just a skull and some spinal cord flopping around on the deck of your ship. They can bake in the Caribbean sun until they become crusty and brittle and literally fall apart on you. Culling your zombie crew from time to time will be necessary in order to maintain optimal fighting strength. (I recommend just tossing them overboard, but if you want to get creative with it—perhaps employing some kind of decommissioning ceremony—then go for it, dude.) Maximum effectiveness of your crew at all times should be

the top priority. While every zombie is different—and, as has been noted, a very diverse selection can be an asset—if a zombie has lost his mast-scaling, skull-splitting, brain-eating "touch," you need to have him replaced forthwith. Zombies who can no longer contribute to the cause have no place in your crew.

"But wait a minute," I hear you saying. "It was easy to raise an undead crew back at that giant pirate graveyard on Hispaniola, but we're in the middle of the ocean now. And also, I think I left my copy of the Necronomicon back on land . . ."

Relax, friend. There are solutions.

Zombies (or have you forgotten?) have the uncanny power to turn humans into zombies like themselves by biting them. In some cases, even a single scratch from a member of the walking dead can lower a human's blood pressure, cast his skin a sickly shade of pale, and turn him into a full-fledged zombie in a matter of hours. The difficulty arises from a zombie's innate, atavistic desire to follow this initial bite with hundreds more in the course of consuming the entire human (or at least his or her brains).

This problem can be navigated, thank goodness, but it will require a bit of intervention on your part.

When you're in the process of overtaking a hostile vessel (be it filled with merchants, enlisted navy men, or fellow pirates) and you espy a particularly hardy and capable sailor and think: "**He** would be good to have on **our** side," mark him and keep a keen eye out for his whereabouts in the coming fracas. If he is truly an accomplished sailor and soldier, then he ought to be one of the last men standing during the ship-to-ship combat. When your zombies have cornered the last remaining humans on the quarterdeck—and they huddle together, ammunition spent, pikes blunted, and swords shattered—you can give these remaining humans a choice.

To do this, I recommend striding forward in dramatic fashion, your cape blowing in the Caribbean breeze and your mustache waxed to perfection. (You too, ladies.) The beleaguered sailors will be so relieved to see a living human that they may be willing to do whatever you say. They will also (if your zombies are doing things right) have already sustained the nicks, scratches, and bites necessary to result in imminent zombification. Your speech, therefore, need not be excessively long or dramatic.

"Ahoy," you might say to them. "You chaps have put up an absolutely smashing fight. Good show! Now, if you'd be kind enough to join me in my captain's quarters for some tea—and perhaps a cocktail—we can discuss next steps."

Little do they know the "next step" will involve you locking them in the brig and waiting for them to turn into zombies. The next morning you unlock the door and, presto change-o, you've got a fresh crop of zombie pirates ready to enlist.

Make this sort of regular replenishment an ongoing thing. Whenever possible, have your zombies bite captured travelers and use local witch doctors to raise pirates from the grave whenever you pull into port.

As a general rule of thumb, if you're on the fence about turning somebody into a zombie, *you should turn him or her into a zombie.* You want to err on the side of more, not less. It's better to have a ship's hold so crammed full of zombies that some may never see the light of day than it is to need some extra zombies in a fight and not have them.

ZOMBIE TIP

The Rotting Man and the Sea . . .

While "sea air" is oft credited with having salutary properties and being good for the body generally, yours will be a crew for which respiration will be entirely optional. To the contrary, your troops can walk underwater, survive in freezing conditions, and relax in relative comfort in a stifling hot ship's hold on a Caribbean July day. (The olfactory conditions for **you,** however, may grow less pleasant as your zombies enter advanced states of decomposition. I recommend keeping aboard some kind of perfume.)

Particularly enterprising zombie pirate captains regularly have the good fortune to reanimate more top-notch zombie pirates than their ship can hold. When this occurs, the best option is usually to maroon them on a small island somewhere easily accessible to you, but without strategic value to anyone else. There, the zombies can wander around harmlessly until you have a use for them. (Wayward travelers discovering the island—and discovering it to be filled with flesh-eating zombies—are unlikely to weigh anchor to investigate. Indeed, your only real concern is "poaching" by other zombie pirate captains, who might be tempted to use your carefully stored undead to reprovision their own ships.)

Rough Seas Ahead!
(A Chapter About Dangerous
Things)

Nobody said this was going to be easy sailing the entire time. I mean, yeah, the zombies in your crew are sort of doing all the real work—all the heavy lifting and that bit—but every zombie pirate captain will face challenges and even dangers. As I hope I've made clear thus far, these dangers will **not** come from European navies or bounty hunters. Any zombie pirate captain worth his or her salt can easily outwit or defeat a European navy ship or pirate. However, zombie pirates are not invincible. There are forces and entities that do pose real, tactile threats to the purse and person of a zombie pirate captain.

Most of these entities will not be attacking you out of chance or consequence. They will not see you as "just another

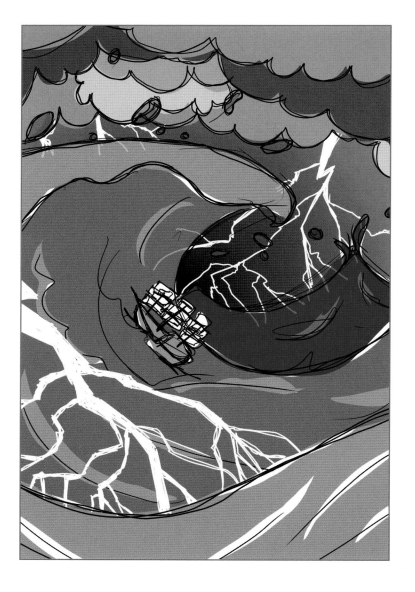

pirate to be brought to justice." Rather, they will have a fundamental problem with your use of zombies for piracy. But—good news!—by employing appropriate countermeasures (and evasive maneuvers), you can avoid these threats and live to plunder another day.

What follows is a brief survey of threats the zombie pirate captain may expect, and instructions as to how they may be neutralized.

Bocors

Bocors (a.k.a.: *bokors, bokos, baycors*) represent the "dark side" of the Voodoo priesthood. (Stop and consider that for a second. This means that within the classification "voodoo priest"—which is already pretty daunting to most people—there is an *even more terrifying and evil subset.* Anyhow, that's these guys.) Bocors are known for putting curses on people, creating the famous voodoo dolls, communicating with the dead . . . and, important for you, *creating zombies.*

Now, most voodoo priests are going to be cool with your being a zombie pirate captain. They'll be happy to help you create a zombie crew as long as they're properly paid for their assistance. Voodoo priests—much like voodoo gods, apparently—respond well to money and gifts. When you pull into port and need your crew replenished, most voodoo priests are going to be happy to help you harvest a new "crop" of zombies for your ship. As long as you're generous with your gold in return, nine times out of ten it's all good. But every now and then you may encounter a bocor. And he is going to be a bit of a grouch.

Bocors seem to view the "dark art" of zombie creation as something inappropriate to trade with outsiders. Bocors feel that zombies should be, in some sense, proprietary to the voodoo priests who have created them. When a bocor finds out that some upstart pirate (who probably doesn't even *practice* voodoo) has raised a zombie crew and is using it to terrorize the Caribbean for his or her own profit . . . Well, let's just say the bocor's going to be very displeased. No, that's putting it lightly. Probably, he will try to destroy you. Fighting a bocor is dangerous business, but sometimes necessary. Your regular playbook is going to have to go out the window for this one. A bocor is a foe that cannot be defeated by ramming your pirate ship into his and sending wave after wave of zombies across his decks. A bocor is just one guy, but he's immensely powerful. To defeat a bocor, you've got to fight *like* a bocor.

They are usually just stringy old men (who don't cut an imposing figure), but this will not be a physical fight. You can leave your weapons at home. Bocors "attack" with curses and spells and by using voodoo spirits with cool-sounding names like Papa Legba, Baron Samedi, and Maman Brigitte.

If left unattended, these curses and spirits can quickly be your undoing. Your zombies will start malfunctioning, your ship will be crushed and destroyed by supernaturally rough seas, and a wide variety of physiological maladies will beset you personally. (Each new ailment will likely be accompanied by a mysterious needle-like stabbing pain.) Your rum will turn to vinegar, your cutlass will rust in its scabbard, and your dreams will be haunted by a mysterious corpse-like figure in a top hat and tails.

When these symptoms begin to present themselves and it becomes apparent that you have fallen into disfavor with a particular bocor, you must act swiftly in order to correct the situation. At the first opportunity, you should pull into port and locate a capable voodoo priest whom you can trust. Explain the situation to him with all speed. The voodoo priest may initially be reluctant to engage a bocor. If this happens, it will be time for you to utilize the one thing that holds sway with all the gods and denizens of the Caribbean. That is **lots and lots and lots of money.**

To your great advantage, nary a set of deities in the world's history has shown such a predilection for treasure—ill-gotten or otherwise—than those in the canon of the voodoo religion. Explain to the hesitant voodoo priest that he *and the spirits he invokes* will be very handsomely paid for their assistance. When he sees the chest brimming with treasure that you have surely brought with you, the priest will instantly understand that you shall be the victor in this exchange and shall have no fear of aiding you.

After altars to the appropriate deities are prepared, open your treasure chest wide so that the voodoo priest can get down to business. (The ceremony that's about to take place may cost you several months' worth of plunder, but trust me, you're getting a bargain.) With access to your loot, the voodoo priest will begin a series of incantations as he begins heaping treasure upon the different altars. While the priest's chantings may be entirely incomprehensible to you, you can be assured that they translate more or less along the following lines: "*Hey there Baron Samedi! How's it goin'? Say, I got a question for you. What did that bocor over in Tobago give you to come after my friend here? Was it a dish full of rum, maybe with some pigs' feet and cigars thrown in for good measure? I'll bet it was. The thing is, my friend is offering you* **a giant pile of rubies** *to forget all about it. He'll even throw in some emeralds and diamonds, just as icing on the cake. How does that sound, Baron? You can continue to chase my man down because someone gave you a little splash of rum back in Tobago, or you can accept this* **huge mound of treasure** *and you don't have to do a thing except let him alone.*"

If you really want to go for extra credit, you can up the amount of treasure and try to convince the spirit in question to go after the bocor who called him up in the first place. However, in most cases, it should suffice simply to be rid of the spirit and its troublesome meddling.

Look, you're going to upset a bocor now and then. As a zombie pirate captain, it's just a fact of life. If you respond to the threat promptly—and are prepared to bribe generously—the potential danger can be negated before anything lasting or dire has been done to your person, ship, or crew.

Religious Missionaries

If bocors represent intrareligious threats to your purse and person, then Christian missionaries represent extrareligious

threats. Missionaries have a way of making things be no fun anymore. They have a habit of identifying lawless, unsettled parts of the world where awesome things are going on (piracy, gambling, fighting, womanizing, voodoo, etc.) and showing up to shut them down.

If the missionaries simply took it upon themselves to do this, it would be little problem for you. (Missionaries are always unarmed. Further, they are frequently unprepared for life in tropical climes, and can be counted upon to be weak from sunburn and fever.) However, missionaries have a way of focusing the attention of the world's churches on the particular awesome area that they've decided to deem unsuitable. They'll arrive in droves and introduce their own ideas to the native populations. Ideas like: "Turning corpses into zombies is 'wrong' and 'evil'" or "Piracy is no career for a respectable bloke" or "The laws of nations ought to be respected at sea as on land."

Talk about a bunch of buzzkills.

Missionaries aren't just lousy to have at parties. They're also dangerous, because if their ideas catch on, then a lot of cool people—**especially zombie pirate captains**—are going to be totally fucked.

Missionaries can convince a population to give up a religion like voodoo. It gradually goes away, and then suddenly you've got nobody left to make zombies for you the next time you want to refit. Your friendly neighborhood voodoo priest has gone and become the cardinal of Hispaniola or something ridiculous, and you're suddenly left in the lurch. While a zombie pirate ship on a bad day can reliably defeat a European navy ship on its best day, zombie pirates cannot defeat **all the ships of all the Christian nations of the world at the same time,** which is precisely who the missionaries would have show up if they can turn the "plight" of a place like the Caribbean into an international cause.

You must not allow that to happen. If the Christian nations of the world begin to show an interest in the areas where you troll, you must convince them that the local residents are "beyond salvation" both physically and spiritually.

Be alert, at all times, for the presence of missionaries in the area. Clues to their presence include hymns being sung on the decks of passing ships, the presence of churches in places where there were no churches before, and a general increase in sobriety and decency among the local populace. Once it has arrived, defeating the missionary scourge is going to take teamwork. There are lots and lots of missionaries being made around the world all the time, and you can't be everywhere at once. Even if you sink all of the missionary-bearing ships you encounter, many will still land in the region and set up camp.

No, to defeat the threatening presence of missionaries, you'll need to use a formidable weapon: education. Specifically, you've got to educate the local populace about the **real** nature of the "new ideas" the missionaries are selling.

In your every interaction with voodoo priests, local residents, or fellow pirates, make clear that the "solution" the missionaries are selling is no kind of solution at all. Sure, it's all hymns and wine drinking at first, but after a while, the missionary religious officials will want the locals to "abandon violence" and make "an honest living" through farming, mining, livestock cultivation, or a thousand other boring occupations. Temperance, abstemiousness, and sobriety will be encouraged, **at least most of the time.** Then, the tithing will begin. (That's right. They want your money. Your money that you worked hard to steal and plunder from other people.)

Encourage residents in your part of the Caribbean not to fall victim to flash-in-the-pan religious fads like "Christianity" that offer a supposed "afterlife" while making life here in the terrestrial world **boring beyond belief.** Point out the ways that they would be far better served by a religion allowing them to excel right now in the actual world where they currently live. And if you want to live forever, then what about just becoming a zombie?

With the proper encouragement, you can convince local populations to reject the seductive advances of European religious missionaries. Cultivate a unified front against them, and the missionaries' efforts will fail. They won't give up instantly, but when they meet with defeat and frustration year after year, they'll suddenly notice that there are places like South America and Africa that are also ripe for the cultivating (and likely a lot less hostile than the pirate- and voodoo-steeped Caribbean is proving).

Get the missionaries interested in heading somewhere else, and the battle is won. Ignore them for too long, and everybody's in trouble.

Other Zombie Pirates

When other pirate captains begin to see how totally awesome and kick-ass your zombie pirate crew is, it's inevitable that a few upstarts are going to want one for themselves. Enterprising imitators may even get as far as beginning the necessary steps and considerations—such as are outlined in the book—to raising a zombie crew. This is unacceptable. There is room in the Caribbean only for one zombie pirate captain at a time, and it should be **you.** Thus, it is incumbent upon you to be ever vigilant against those who would seek to emulate your particular route to success. Flatterers and sycophants are one thing (and may even be fun to have around), but copycats are a serious problem.

To begin fortifying yourself against other zombie pirates, keep your ear to the ground. You know better than anybody that a ship full of zombie pirates doesn't just "suddenly happen." It is the result of weeks or months of meticulous preparation. Your best bet for preventing zombie pirate competitors is to stop them before they really get started.

Now, as a member of the Caribbean underworld in the 1700s, you're not going to be the only person interested in having some zombies created for your personal use. People who just want a zombie or two around the house to help with the washing are not a concern. It's larger numbers of zombies that should make your ears prick up. If you hear about locals who have placed exceptionally large orders with the local voodoo priests, see if you can find out what's up. More times than not, the use for these zombies may prove to be entirely legitimate (at least by your standards). Sugarcane plantation owners may be seeking a loyal workforce for their fields. Limestone mine magnates may be looking for workers who don't get all "up in arms" or "even care at all" every time the canary dies. Unpopular officials in local governments may be seeking a secret army of undead strongmen they can use to quell popular uprisings against them. These scenarios are liable to happen now and then, and should be no great cause for concern.

If large numbers of zombies are being ordered—especially in port towns or places where pirates are known to be—and nobody can quite account for how they might be used, then you need to take an interest in it right away. A competing zombie pirate crew may be brewing. Likewise, if you find evidence of zombie creation focused specifically on burying grounds where pirates are known to be interred, it should raise a red flag.

Has that used-ship salesman finally unloaded that termite-eaten, shot-to-hell bark that you thought he kept on the lot just as some sort of joke? You need to follow up and find out the details. (Act impressed and flatter him to loosen his tongue. After all, he must be quite a salesman if he unloaded *that* boat, right?) If the ship dealer reveals that some high school kids just pooled their money and bought it to go crash it into some rocks for fun, you have nothing to worry about. If an intense young man or woman with a piratical mien—but, mysteriously, no crew to speak of—bought the ship as though its deteriorated condition were an *asset*, then you might want to find out where it's moored and go get more information.

It is a sign of a more *advanced* problem if you begin to hear reports of sightings of a zombie pirate vessel other than your own. Even at this point, if you act quickly, all hope is not lost. A novice zombie pirate captain will get a lot of things wrong at first. The most common mistake a novice captain makes is to underestimate the sheer number of zombies he ought to have onboard. Many captains believe that when they've "recruited" as many zombie pirate crew members as human crew members are needed to run a pirate ship, their job is done! It does not occur to them that zombies are likely to be destroyed in battle with a greater frequency than human pirates, and nothing prevents them from filling the hold of their ship with "backup" zombies. (Backup zombies may apparently "serve no purpose" when the ship is just sailing around the Caribbean, but, as you well know, the moment the fighting starts it will become strikingly apparent why having a bunch of extra zombies is not only advisable but *necessary* to victory at sea.) If this is the case, and you have the sense that the competing zombie pirate captain is still getting his sea legs, you can put him away. Not personally, of course, but you can have someone tip off a local navy that "one of those zombie pirates" is around and in a vulnerable condition. The local navies will be so sick of reporting defeats at the hands of a zombie pirate (you) that they'll be fools if they don't jump at the chance to engage one they actually have a shot at defeating. If things go as they should, the European navy will likely show up the fight with a surplus of battleships, and the neophyte zombie pirate—presuming himself invincible—will be woefully undermanned (or underzombied, as the case may be). The European navy gets to report a rare victory against a zombie pirate, and you have your competition eliminated for you. Everybody wins (except the other zombie pirate).

If you do find yourself in a worst-case scenario—ship to ship with another zombie pirate with an undead crew as big as your own—you'd better be prepared to get your hands dirty. Zombies won't attack other zombies, at least not in hand-to-hand combat. After a couple of opening cannon salvoes, it's going to come down to a game of one-on-one: you versus the competing zombie pirate captain. (Let's just hope that the months at sea as commander of a crew of zombies haven't made you soft and fat. That's the really lousy thing about competing zombie pirate captains; once they get going, you're going to have to get off your duff and take care of them yourself.) If you anticipate a showdown with a fully matured zombie pirate captain, brush up your pistol and cutlass skills, because that's how things are getting settled.

Sea Monsters

Finally, but not insignificantly, we come to the rubbery, many-tentacled problem of sea monsters.

The ocean is a wide and mysterious place. Its depths remain largely unseen, despite the best efforts of science.

Its deep-sea crevasses and caverns provide places where unusual (and dangerous) entities can evolve without interruption for thousands of years. (I'm not saying that *all* of it is full of monsters, but parts of it definitely are.)

Sea monsters come in a variety of shapes, but are united by their size (which is "very big"). In many cases, a small sea monster would just be called a "fish" or "squid." It is gigantic proportion that earns a creature the title of "monster." It is also this quality that makes it dangerous to your ship and crew.

Some sea monsters are fish or sharks of biblical proportions which can swim underneath a pirate vessel and surface, lifting

the ship out of the water entirely. Others are many-armed monstrosities whose very tentacles have tentacles. (Sea monsters of this variety are well known for their tendency to latch onto a ship and pull it down to its destruction.) Other sea monsters look like a giant snake and can constrict a ship with its body while simultaneously attacking crew members on deck with its head. Others still can come in the form of gelatinous sea-blobs—a sort of sentient marine offal that desires to envelop a pirate ship like aspic around a lark's tongue.

Sea monsters seem to be especially attuned to the presence of zombie pirates. Perhaps they can sense the supernatural concentration of so many reanimated corpses. Whatever the reason for their attunement, it is clear that sea monsters are gunning for zombie pirates. However, with a little preparation, you should be able to extricate yourself (literally and figuratively) from their grips with reliable success.

To defeat a sea monster, it is essential to first ask the question: "What does a sea monster want?" When it has attached itself to your ship and is eating your zombies one by one, it's tempting to answer: "Well, to eat us, obviously." Go deeper. **Why** does it want to eat you? It's not because wooden sailing ships are delicious. They're wood. It's not because zombies are a good source of nutrition. Zombies are rotting and infested with weevils and maggots. (That's not going to taste good, even for something used to living on gunk from under the ocean.) Sea creatures could much more easily get a good meal by trolling the depths with their mouths open instead of taking the time and effort to attack zombie pirate ships.

Sea monsters want to be famous. **That's** their problem, and **that's** why they'll attack you.

Did you ever notice how sea monsters are always referred to as "the legendary" or "the great" or "the terrible"? This is not an accident. Sea monsters behave as they do *for the very purpose* of securing themselves a place in the history of famous creatures. Attacking ships is hard, dangerous work, but sea creatures do it anyway because they know it can make them famous. A sea creature's only concern is furthering its own reputation.

When you show up—the famous zombie pirate captain in his famous ship full of zombie pirates—any sea monster noting you is going to be filled with rage and envy. It may attack you simply out of spite and hate, or for the usual purpose of increasing its fame—in this case, by defeating the "undefeatable" zombie pirate captain. (Getting famous by killing somebody famous is a tried-and-true technique that has worked for sea monsters for millennia.)

Insanely, the annals of great maritime explorers are full of examples of captains faced with a sea monster who tried to defeat it through force of arms. Maybe they—like the sea monsters—were obsessed with fame and thought that by defeating a legendary monster they'd make their name known far and wide. Maybe they were just stupid. (Because they aren't around anymore to ask, I doubt we'll ever know.) For whatever reason, many of the best and brightest in the seagoing world have decided to take on sea monsters. None have ever succeeded.

Let's face it: **You** are not going to defeat a sea monster with might or magic. No crew of pirate zombies—however fierce and slavering—is going to take on a turtle with human intelligence that's two hundred feet high. No voodoo charm or shaman's spell is going to work quickly enough to counter the fifty giant tentacle arms that are tearing your ship to pieces. (I don't care how good a shot you are with that pistol—hitting a giant squid right in the eyeball is a ridiculously hard shot, and nine times out of ten just makes it madder.)

Nope. When a sea monster rears its ugly head (or heads), you've got only one real shot to save the situation. (No, it's not going to end with a well-placed harpoon, so you can just stop thinking along those lines altogether.)

If the monster is tall and sticks out of the water, climb to the highest point on your ship. If it stays low—like a bed of wriggling tentacles—then lower yourself to its level in a dinghy.

Next, address the creature directly. (You will not need to introduce yourself, in all likelihood, your ship being known on sight as that of a famous zombie pirate captain.) Ask the creature if he's heard of you. Then, before it can angrily respond, tell the creature that **you** have heard of **him!** Tell the giant creature that you've heard it's been up to some really impressive monsterin'. Tell it everybody's talking about how large and monstrous it is.

Then, before it occurs to the creature to build on this reputation by sinking you—which is what it was going to do anyway—propose a partnership. Let it know that you think that maybe, just maybe, it is "cool" and "down" enough to hang with your crew. Not

ZOMBIE TIP

Shiver Me Timbers . . .

When your timbers are shivering, it's not a good thing. It means that your boat is about to physically shake apart (usually because you've run it into something like land, an iceberg, or another ship). "Shiver me timbers" is just a nautical way of saying "I'll be fucked." If you become successful enough as a zombie pirate, maybe sea captains will start saying "Eat me brains!" instead, because some things are even worse than running your ship into an iceberg. You've just gotta, y'know, get them out there more.

literally, of course. (I mean, who wants to actually spend time with a sea monster? And what're you going to do together?) Still, you should invite this fame-seeking behemoth to become an unofficial member of your crew.

If you do this correctly, and shout loudly enough, the creature should at least pause from its attack on your ship and begin to mull the idea over. This pause is where you should really start laying it on thick. Tell the monster about all the fun things you and your crew get to do. Tell it about all the ink you get in the European broadsheets, and the exclusive zombie pirate parties you host once a year on your secret Caribbean island, with wine and wenches and bobbing for diamonds the size of your fist. Don't act excited, though. Come off as "too cool for school," like these parties actually bore you. Tell the monster they're "just okay."

If you play your cards right, the sea monster will be loath to turn down any partnership that looks as though it can make the creature more famous, exclusive, and legendary. Rather than attacking you, it will show the greatest alacrity to flatter you, help you, and ingratiate itself to you. Only thus can a sea monster be defeated.

Vampirates, and
How to Deal with Them

That's right, vampirates. You thought you had a monopoly on the undead at sea.

There is another scourge on the water. A force no less lethal to sea travelers than zombies, and no less feared. These are the nocturnal pirates who are also vampires. They are the **vampirates.**

Originally spilling from the Black Sea (the Romanian coast to be precise), and spreading into the Aegean, the Mediterranean, and eventually across the Atlantic to the Caribbean, vampirates are an annoying bit of competition that you may have to deal with now and again. If you are prepared, you can reliably send vampirates packing every time they show up.

Vampirates are not listed among the entities that threaten zombie pirates, because they never attack zombies. Your ship of zombie pirates has but one living human on it—you. Thus, you are something of a low-value target as far as vampirates are concerned. They would much rather wait for a trade ship laden with nice yummy traders and travelers than pick through a thousand bony zombies just to get to you. However, like all vampires, vampirates **will** defend themselves if attacked. If you see them, you **are** going to attack them. . . .

Zombies and vampires have always represented polar opposites in the monster kingdom. They have never liked one another and have never cooperated. It is only natural that their ancient annoyance with one another should spill over into the seas.

Vampires like to lay claim to being the more naturally (or "unnaturally") suited to being pirates. For example (say the vampires), they:

- Are already flamboyant dressers, so the earrings, vests, and other affectations of piracy come naturally to them. (Many vampirates arrive for their first day at sea already decked out in scarves, jewels, and superfluous eyepatches.)

- Are already in tune with animal familiars—being able to command wolves, bats, and other creatures. Thus, as pirates, they can have remarkably in-depth psychic relationships with the parrots that festoon their shoulders.
- Feed efficiently upon the blood of captured sailors, **but also** have great affection for the finer things in life and for displays of great wealth. Thus, vampires are the "perfect pirates" because they lust equally for the blood of the living and for their things.
- Can, under certain circumstances, fly. (Which is good if you fall overboard and don't want to get wet . . .)

Also, like zombies, vampires are remarkably tough to kill (requiring a "heartshot" the way zombies require a headshot). Neither can a zombie or vampire be suffocated or drowned.

But vampires have a way of conveniently forgetting that there are many ways in which they are **not at all** adapted for a life of piracy. These are things the vampires won't tell you. They include:

- An inability to function during daylight hours. (This is the big one, obviously, and is almost crippling to the vampirates' chances of landing the best treasure-laden merchant ships. It's hard enough to see the tiny speck on the horizon that can end up being a high-value target **during the day.** It's nearly impossible at night. Most of a vampirate's successes will come from dumb luck— their ship simply drifting in the right place at the right time and running into a merchant ship.) And if the pirates are *attacked themselves* during daylight hours, they're in big, big trouble. For this reason, some vampirates maintain a skeleton crew of humans to man their ship during the day and evade aggressors.

- A need to be at the center of attention whenever possible. Vampires are notorious publicity whores. They like to live in beautiful castles and host fancy dinner parties. Unlike zombies (who can just eat a bunch of people and then go home), vampires need to have their exploits recorded in novels, songs, and sequential art. In a career (piracy) where your very whereabouts should be a closely guarded secret, a lust for fame is less of a benefit than a liability.

- A general daintiness and disdain for "getting their hands dirty." What is life aboard a pirate ship if not a series of invitations to be soaked by the brine of the sea, covered in bird droppings and the sweat of your colleagues, and to get a coating of gunpowder under your fingernails? Vampires want to keep their hands clean and their waistcoat and stockings unblemished. They want to avoid dirt and grime generally. (It may seem odd that someone who is already undead should manage to be so germ-phobic, but there you are.) Zombies, in sharp contrast to vampires, come to the job with pre-dirtied hands covered with a good caking of charnel earth.

Should vampirates show up in waters where you're trolling, you should consider them a menace to be dealt with promptly. In addition to being another competitor for you to contend with, vampirates lower the standards for the aquatic undead collectively. Their fancy clothes and effete tastes give people the wrong impression. You'd better take them on, lest the colonials believe that some kind of pirate tea party is going down.

Here are the ways of engaging a vampirate ship (which probably has some clever name like the *Bat* or *Carpathian*). Consider these approaches carefully, weighing the benefits and drawbacks, before proceeding.

The Lure and Attack

This is optimal if you happen to surprise a vampirate ship during daylight hours. All undead crew members will be belowdecks, sleeping in coffins buried in a giant pit of graveyard dirt (and you thought the insides of zombie pirate ships were weird places). The ship will be manned by a skeleton crew of humans who are probably under the magical influence of the sleeping vampires. However, no matter how strong this influence may be—for there are reports that it can approach downright possession—the vampirates will **not** be able to emerge from their slumbers and defend themselves until the sun goes down.

As with any zombie pirate engagement, you want to attach yourself to the enemy ship with grappling hooks and send your zombies aboard. However, unlike in engagements with typical ships, you must avoid a head-on approach. The crew manning the vampirate ship has been given the order to run like hell from anything and everything that approaches it during daylight hours. (Nothing good can happen to a vampire during the day.) Because of their weakness to sunlight and their need to evade things, the vampirate ship will be engineered for speed. Your zombie pirate ship is **not** built for speed. If you try to chase a vampirate ship down, it will run from you until sunset, at which point some very cranky vampirates will emerge from the hold and probably want a word with you.

The human crew on a vampirate ship is tasked with doing more than steering clear of things during daylight hours. It is also charged with keeping an eye out for prey that can be followed during the day and attacked at night. Through this strategy, **you** will transform your ship into vampirate prey.

During daylight hours, steer past the vampirate vessel as if your craft is broken. Go very slowly. Make it clear that something is wrong with your ship. Your sails. Your rudder. Something.

Transform your deck from a zombie pirate war vessel to that of some rich, defenseless humans out for a Sunday cruise. Get your most human-looking zombies together and disarm them, dress them like wealthy travelers—bonnets and waist-coats are recommended, and jewelry is compulsory—and let them wander around on the deck. The humans manning the vampirate ship will not be able to resist following such a prize.

Let the vampirate ship follow you. Allow it to draw close. See if you can get it to pull alongside you. **Then** launch the grappling hooks.

Once your ship is tethered to theirs—and the proper zombies (the ones with rapiers and rotting faces) spring out from their hiding places—the crew of the vampirate ship is going to realize too late that it has made a massive error in judgment. Your zombies will storm their decks and dispatch the scant human crew with little difficulty. Then **you** can go below and eliminate the vampirates personally.

(When staking vampirates, it's awesome to use wooden stakes you've hacked from the mast of their own ship. It sort of says: "I couldn't even be bothered to come prepared. I just used what I found onboard, and now you're getting staked **by a piece of your own boat**!" You can really see the anger and annoyance in the vampirates' eyes in that one moment when they wake up and hiss as the stake is driven through their hearts. Awesome.)

The Fabulous Party

As noted, vampirates are suckers for the fancy and frilly. They are notoriously unable to resist invitations to masquerade balls in Hispaniola ports, and many a vamp has met his undoing by staying out till dawn in hopes of securing a mention in the local society pages. While you do not have easy access to a printing press to start minting issues of the *Dramatic Vampyre Weeklie*, you **can** throw an irresistibly fantastic party aboard your ship—a fantastic party where the vampires die at the end. This tactic calls for a more dramatic transformation of your ship and its crew, but is a completely delightful way to kill vampires, and so you may find it more than worth the extra effort.

The first goal, in the Fabulous Party, is to turn your ship into a floating masquerade ball. Hire musicians, decorate your decks, and festoon your zombies in the fanciest finery and most undead-concealing face powder and ornate masks. Hang so many candles from your sails that your ship becomes a floating beacon of revelry. If you are near a port city, invite aboard magistrates, merchants, and other local celebrities to give it an added touch of authenticity. (Try to keep your zombies from eating them until after the vampires are dealt with, though.)

When the musicians strike up the tunes, the guests (and zombies) begin to dance, and the sounds of dainty revelry begin to spill out over the sea, the vampirates will be able to hear it from miles away. (Don't worry about knowing where exactly the vampires are. If they're in the same sea as you, they'll use their supernatural powers to make sure that swift winds carry them to your party before the third quadrille of the evening is through.)

When the vampirate ship pulls alongside, welcome your new guests aboard with all deference. Offer them refreshments and invite them to take part in the festivities. (Make sure you tether your ship to theirs so that you can plunder it later.)

As the evening drags on, begin to circulate a rumor. Tell people that in the captain's quarters, it's like a vampire V.I.P. room. All the coolest and most dramatic vampires are in there. Dracula, Lestat, Edward Cullen—it turns out they're all are aboard and chillin' in this ultraexclusive area. As word spreads across the deck of your ship, the vampirates will start wondering whose neck they have to bite to get invited inside.

You should be standing at the door to the captain's quarters, acting as a kind of bouncer.

"It's kind of crowded in there right now," you can tell the vampirates as they anxiously begin to form a queue. "We're trying to keep it balanced. Too many undead right now. You'll have to wait just a minute, guys."

The vampirates will almost certainly try to ply you with gifts, or claim to be "great friends" with someone in Dracula's entourage. You must resist these entreaties. Only admit one or two vampirates at a time.

As you have no doubt guessed, Dracula is not waiting inside the cabin to regale them with fascinating stories about the time he and Jonathan Harker got totally wasted. No. Instead, your vampirate visitors will be met with a room full of zombies armed with stakes and specially trained to stab for the heart.

As the party progresses, make sure vampirates keep entering the V.I.P. room and not leaving. When all of them are in that totally exclusive, cool place (which turns out to be vampire heaven, or whatever) you can just call off the ball, have your zombies eat the rest of the human guests, and sack the vampirates' ship.

The Inauthentic Aspirant

Do you like to do the important things yourself? Are you a real "personal touch" kind of leader? Do you like to see the pain, disappointment, and anguish in the eyes of your enemies each time they are defeated?

If you've answered "yes" to these questions, then you may want to use the Inauthentic Aspirant to take on the vampirates in your neck of the Caribbean. When it is not enough that your enemies be defeated, but must also feel personally betrayed by someone close to them, the Inauthentic Aspirant is the way to go. (Who would blame you, right? Fucking vampires . . . Thinking they get to be pirates . . .)

As entities that consider themselves to be at the apex of desirability and drama, it is only natural that vampires should expect others to want to be like them. Using the Inauthentic Aspirant, you will meet these expectations.

First things first. Find the vampirates. Approach them in the middle of the night when they are in their element. Sail up to them slowly and visibly. Pull your ship alongside theirs and hail them. Expect a conversation that runs along the following lines:

You: "Hey there!"

Vampirate: "Eww, zombies. Dirty, smelly zombies. They do things without a touch of elegance or class. They probably can't even spell 'monogrammed handkerchief.'"

You: "Wait, I'm not a zombie! I'm human. I'm a zombie pirate captain."

Vampirate: "Is there just one of you, then? Hardly worth getting out of the grave, is it?"

You: "Look, I'm here because you guys are *so cool* and I want to *be like you.*"

Vampirate: "Go on . . ."

You: "It's just . . . I've been a zombie pirate captain, and a pretty successful one—you might have heard of me—but I've always dreamed of being a vampirate. Everybody knows vampirates are the most interesting pirates out there. I mean, me and all the other pirates, we're always talking about you. Wondering what you're up to. Guessing which of you might be dating each other. Appending drawings of you to the inside of our cabin walls, and then sort of looking at them and sighing."

Vampirate: "Understandable. Tell me more."

You: "Well, it's become clear to me that vampiracy is the way to go. Why am I dicking around here with all these awesome, brain-eating zombies when I could be, you know, putting my hand to my forehead and sighing dramatically, looking unhealthily pale, and spending all my time attending to the management of an inconvenient blood disease?"

Vampirate: "You do make a good case."

You: "Yeah, so, I'm just here trying to see what I need to do to prove myself worthy to join up. Do you think you could clue me in?"

This entreaty will set the vampirate to thinking. You see, like zombies, vampires sometimes just kill their victims, but also sometimes bite them to turn them undead. Unlike zombies, who usually create other zombies accidentally—like by biting the finger of a human who was too quick and escaped—vampires usually make a point of only admitting others to their "clique" who appear to have the requisite qualities (drama, self-absorption, a penchant for capes). I say "usually" because vampires are especially susceptible to flattery. Don't worry if you don't see "vampire material" when you look in the mirror. Vampires love flattery, and are always willing to make exceptions regarding whom they admit to their nocturnal fraternity. (Or should that perhaps be "sorority"? I'm just saying.)

Anyhow, if you follow the conversational outline above, you will almost certainly be invited aboard the vampirate ship and brought as an initiate before the captain. (Try not to laugh when you are introduced to the world-weary blood addict who fancies himself your equal upon the seas.) Continue to act as though you are honored and awed to be in the presence of such legendary maritime warriors. Beg to be allowed to apprentice yourself on their boat as a member of their human skeleton crew. Ask to be given the chance to prove yourself worthy of one day joining their ranks as a full-fledged vampirate. Lay it on thick. Be dramatic. (Kissing the hem of his cloak can be a nice added touch. Asking for an autograph is a good one, too.)

Once the vampirate captain relents and allows that you *may* one day prove yourself worthy of vampiracy, show great eagerness to serve as the lowest member of his ship's crew. (Don't worry if they make you a first-class scum-scrubber who answers to the cook. The lower, the better, and the more dramatic your eventual betrayal.)

Now you're serving as one of the few human crew members aboard a vampirate ship. Once you've secured this perma-nent job, it's really up to you how long you want to drag it out. (I didn't say this was the fastest way to get rid of a ship of vampirates, but it may be the most satisfying.) If you really want to make them suffer, endear yourself to the vampirates as much as possible. Leave them thoughtful little "vampire gifts"—like bloody human hearts on Valen-tine's Day—to let them know you care. Listen attentively as the vampirate captain invites you his quarters for a blood cocktail and talks long into the night about his early days as a novice vampirate. Launder their doublets and have them hanging up and ready for the vampirates as they emerge from their coffins each evening.

Then, one day when they least expect it, strike, quite literally, at their hearts.

The day should begin just like any other, with you giving every appearance of happily enjoying another day of servitude as lackey to a bunch of self-absorbed parasites. Then, as dawn breaks, stalk the deck with ninja-like skill and dispatch the other members of the human crew one by one.

After that, you may proceed below and stake the vampirates one by one as they sleep in their coffins.

Leave one "alive." Word will reach other vampirates of how their kind are dealt with in the Caribbean. It will be a long, long time before any vampirates dare to return.

Romances and Ransoms

One thing about piracy is that you're in it for the money. That, basically, is the reason for the season. You're out here to take money from other people's boats and put it on your boat. Also, they get killed (by zombies!) and you don't.

That's not to say that you're nothing more than a cold-hearted capitalist with a belt full of pistols and a crew of several hundred walking corpses. You have the same needs and desires as any man (or woman), and unlike the zombies who stumble about listlessly on the deck of your ship, you still have functioning genitals.

In short, the time may arise when you find yourself desiring romance on the high seas. The Caribbean is a beautiful place,

after all, and the ships that you capture are likely to be filled with buxom wenches and strapping young sailors, nicely tanned and appropriately proportioned. You would not be the first pirate to be tempted by the flesh of others. Though pirate captains are often portrayed as solitary adventurers, some of piracy's biggest names have found romance at sea. Blackbeard is, by some accounts, reckoned as having as many as fourteen wives **at the same time!** Anne Bonny and Calico Jack Rackham are two pirates who fell in love with one another. Countless others have enjoyed frequent dalliances with attractive seafarers whom they encountered in the course of sacking ships.

However, romance is not the only reason that a pirate might elect to spare a captured person during a raid on a ship. Another reason is kidnapping.

Again, you're out here to make money, right? Right. So when you've captured a merchant vessel, taken all the gold from its hold, plundered all the banknotes from the captain's strongbox, and pulled every piece of jewelry off of every finger aboard, don't think for a moment that you've plumbed all the revenue streams available to you. Though you may have left them stunned and naked on the deck (and trembling in fear before a mob of slavering zombies), some of these captives can still provide you with opportunities for monetary gain.

You need not concern yourself with the lowborn and servile. They may be thrown to the zombies with all haste. (Although a scullery maid or novice seaman might be ransomed for a small sum of money, it is unlikely to be worth the time and coin you'll spend keeping them alive in the interim.) Those descending from a royal bloodline (or at least a wealthy bloodline) are another matter entirely.

Holding rich Europeans for ransom can be an *exceedingly* profitable undertaking. Further, if the captive in question *is* of a royal heritage, then ransoming him or her will be a

> **ZOMBIE TIP:**
> **The Motion of the Ocean . . .**
>
> Luckily for zombie pirate captains, zombies are entirely sexless creatures. They will not waste your time with the pursuit of sweethearts, courtship, or other flights of love and/or lust. Oh sure, zombies may retain physical characteristics denoting gender, but the zombification process seems to involve a complete erasure of a reanimated person's sex drive. Either that, or eating brains is just *so* much better than sex that zombies simply can't be bothered with it anymore. Brains are just *that* good. (Kinda makes you curious to try eating brains, doesn't it?)

wonderful way to upset and aggrieve the annoying European superpowers that so inveterately hunt you. Through an effective kidnapping, the king of Spain will come to know you not just as "that annoying zombie pirate who attacks all my ships" but also "that annoying zombie pirate who attacks all my ships *and kidnapped my niece*!"

What about that niece? One of the rules of kidnapping—maybe the only one, actually—is that you agree to keep the kidnapped person alive until the ransom is paid. The mechanics of accomplishing this aboard a ship crowded with flesh-hungry zombies can be daunting. You will need to confine your captive to someplace secure, like your personal quarters. Then, as the weeks of waiting go by, maybe the two of you get to be friends. Then maybe you get to be more than friends. Then you've got an age-old dilemma.

You would not be the first pirate to become romantic with someone you initially planned to ransom. In fact, if you do decide to go the holding-people-for-ransom-route, I'd say you can probably count on it happening at least once or twice.

Now, I'm not one to insist that the past *always* predicts the future, but there seem to be some pretty consistent patterns for the way these things work out. In most cases:

- The captive and captor fall in love and marry. The captive forsakes her royal bloodline and the chance to be the ruler of a superpower in favor of a life on a crowded, smelly pirate ship with someone they "love." The captive may even elect to become a pirate him- or herself.

- The captive's love for the captor turns out to be less than genuine and is actually part of a ruse designed to facilitate escape. One night, after a romantic cruise around Tortuga, the pirate looks away for a second and his or her beloved is jumping overboard and swimming for dry land.

- The captive's love for the captor turns out to be less than genuine and is part of an intricately complicated plot to *exact revenge* on the pirate captain for killing the captive's father/mother/sister/brother many years before. The captor can expect to be stabbed in the middle of the night or to have poison slipped into his or her drink.

- The captor was once a slave owned by the captive— before becoming a pirate—so you've got a delicious world-turned-upside-down sort of situation. Though they may be attracted to one another, the real novelty of the arrangement comes from this power reversal. (Plus there's the whole master/slave sexual dynamic turning things up in the bedroom. Reowr.)

If you decide to go the kidnapping route, don't be surprised if you end up with one of these outcomes. Obviously, you don't want to get your throat slashed, but then again, maybe you find true love (or at least get enough nooky that your zombies stop looking good to you for a while). This one is all up to you, friend.

A Bounty on
Your Head

Having a bounty on your head is not something that concerns a successful pirate. In fact, if you **don't** have a bounty on your head in your first few months of piracy, you're doing something wrong.

What does a bounty mean when you really stop and look at it?

- You have upset European and colonial powers.
- You have upset local governments.
- Your actions are **so** deleterious to the interests of these powers and governments that it would be worth a considerable sum of money to be rid of you.

Correctly considered, these are all good things. They indicate that you are becoming an accomplished and effective zombie pirate. In fact, the larger the amount of money offered for bringing you to justice—and the more countries/governments/shipping interests offering it—the better!

When you're a zombie pirate with a bounty on your head, there are usually just two categories of people who are going to come after you. The first is people who "have to"—this includes European navy ships and local privateers (a.k.a. other pirates) that have agreed to help bring you to justice. You have very little to fear from this first group. After you have established yourself as the dominant pirate of the region (which all zombie pirate captains naturally are), nobody in his right mind is going to want to attack you. Other pirates may cut privateering deals where they agree to help hunt you down, but none of them actually want to do it. (The agreement is just a PR move with the local governments, if anything.) European navies will soon be frightened of you, and will use any excuse in the manual (and some that aren't) to avoid engaging you if at all possible.

So, really, this leaves just the other category that responds to a bounty: armed ships **from outside the Caribbean.** Though the Caribbean totally rules—and there are a million reasons why you'd **never** want to leave it—there's a great big world out there, full of ships and enterprising crews who've never dealt with you before. When word reaches the North American colonies or the Viceroyalty of New Grenada that there is a literal ton of money to be made by hunting down some pirate with a shipful of zombies, all kind of comers may show up. They may even see your crew full of zombies as part of the attraction. ("Zombies move slowly, don't they? And are stupid and stuff, right? How hard could this be?") This mercenary is going to forget the other side of the coin. Namely, that zombies don't feel fear, retreat, die when you shoot them through the heart, or drown when they fall overboard.

> **ZOMBIE TIP:**
>
> **When a bounty is not a mutiny . . .**
>
> Those new to the world of piracy may have heard of something called "mutiny on the Bounty" and incorrectly consider it as involving a bounty on a pirate's head. This phrase confuses many, as it actually references a mutiny aboard a British Royal Navy ship that was **named** the *Bounty,* and not a bounty on a pirate*.* The *Bounty* had originally been a coal ship named *Bethia*, so when the Royal Navy bought it and refitted it as a military ship, maybe they felt like they had to give it a new badass name too. Whatever the reason, it has confused pirates and zombie pirates for years.

Though they will likely pose little to no threat to your zombie pirate crew, these annoying interlopers can take up your valuable time. Also, other than feeding your crew of zombies with their brains, there is no benefit to defeating these mercenaries. After all, they're mercenaries because they **want** to get money, and not because they **have** money. Pillaging their ship after the battle is unlikely to reveal anything of use or value.

Thus, it's best to avoid engagements with these bounty-seeking chumps whenever possible. There's just no upside to engaging them. As a zombie ship, stealth and fleeing will not be your strong suits. That being the case, your best bet may be to confuse the bounty hunters.

When they draw near and prepare to fire, you can run up a white flag of truce. Then, when they come close to meet with you, you can be like: "That bounty? It *totally* got called off. Like, months ago, I think. Now we've got a truce with the French Navy. It's all good."

And if you learn that more than one bounty-hunting ship is in the area looking for you, then you can just come up with a bounty of your own. If the British are offering 5,000 gold sovereigns for the destruction of your ship, offer a bounty hunter 6,000 for every **other bounty hunter** he destroys. Are the Spanish offering 3,500 *reals* for your head? Then make it an even 4,000 for **the heads of those pursuing you.** This is called "subcontracting" and will save you lots of time and hassle. Get the bounty hunters fighting among themselves before you bother tangling with them yourself.

You're a zombie pirate. You've got more important things to do.

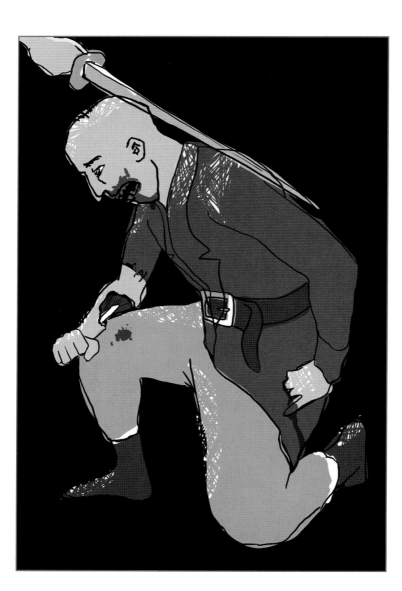

Appointing
Your Seconds

While some degree of micromanagement is always necessary when supervising zombies, every pirate captain has to delegate some of his or her tasks to others. Nothing would get done if a captain has to do it all personally. A captain needs to create a hierarchy. He or she needs to select a second in command—or maybe a few seconds in command—who can handle things when shit gets busy.

Pirate ships are big, busy, complicated places—especially during sea battles—and you can't be everywhere at once. If you're at the bow, you're not going to be able to see what's going on at the stern when the cannonballs start flying. Just as you have divided your zombies into categories based on the specialized tasks that they can (or can't) perform, you may wish to appoint **especially** high-functioning zombies as your seconds in command.

A quick review of zombie functionality is in order.

The average zombie can moan or say a word or two, and is easily distracted and confused. A more exclusive subset of zombies, however, may be able to speak entire sentences and may have the intelligence to avoid basic obstacles between it and its target. A more exclusive subset still may be able to read signs, understand basic commands, and interact with tools and machines. It is this final category of zombie—the most high-functioning zombies—from which you should begin to select your seconds.

The Code of Zombie Piracy prescribes that you appoint several "seconds." While the wits left inside their rotting heads will be no match for your own (or come anywhere close), these zombies *are* able to make very basic decisions that will, in turn, allow you to delegate some of the decision-making around the ship. For example, these higher-functioning zombie seconds can:

- Judge when enemy ships are in range of cannon, and give the order to fire.
- Notice when two ships are almost touching one another and lay down planks or ropes to connect them.
- Open doors to allow more zombies to spill across the decks.
- Operate sails and rigging according to your direction.

There will not be many zombies like this in the entire Caribbean. You want to make sure you have as many as possible on your ship. By taking just a few moments to appoint these zombies your seconds, you will streamline your operations both in and out of combat.

ZOMBIE TIP:

The circle of trust . . .

Some qualities should disqualify even the highest-functioning (almost human) zombies from a place in your inner circle of trust. For example, if a zombie's been putrefying in some slag pit for years and has an especially horrible smell, you're not going to want to keep it around and give it orders, no matter how unusually smart it seems. Zombies that are subject to a physical handicap that makes them prohibitively difficult to work with—like being impaled on a giant wooden spike that they now just drag around constantly—are also not good candidates. Also, watch out for zombies that have uncontrollable predilections toward violence. If a high-functioning zombie loses the ability to pay attention to you or obey your commands the moment a ship of tasty humans pulls into sight, then, yeah, he's basically useless.

Privateering

Who do zombies work for? Who do pirates work for?

No, not "nobody," smart guy.

If you look closely, the world is full of examples of both zombies and pirates appearing to be in the employ of numerous entities external to themselves.

Wealthy European plantation owners have long histories of employing zombies as footmen, servants, and sugarcane millworkers. Unsavory political functionaries in colonial Caribbean outposts have sometimes seen the local voodoo priest about acquiring a zombie's services to assassinate local rabble-rousers who are troublesome to them. Provincial dictators have even used zombies to quell peasant uprisings.

Pirates, too, have found themselves in the employ of others, usually as privateers. Privateering can take many forms, but in the Caribbean it mostly takes shape as one European power giving pirates the green light to attack and rob ships sailing under the flag of other nations. Essentially, pirates agreed to be deputized and do the "dirty work" of helping one European navy fight against another.

Needless to say, **both zombie and pirate employment relationships tend to have problems.**

Virtually no record exists of a person who successfully caused zombies to show fealty to a political cause. To the contrary, history has shown that one who would involve zombies in a quest for empire **is almost always undone by those very same zombies.** Enterprising and unscrupulous plantation owners who have sought to employ zombies in their factories and fields as "miracle employees" who never need to be fed, clothed, or rested usually find themselves dying in horrible/highly comic ways at the hands of zombies who have mistaken them for sacks of sugarcane and accordingly thrown them, kicking and screaming, into a grinder. Colonial mayors who recruit zombies to assassinate their enemies and political opponents frequently find that their enemies have **also** employed zombies—and for the same purpose. Thus, it becomes like a boxing match where both opponents knock one another out at the same time. The zombies succeed in their missions, leaving everyone involved dead. (Invariably in these cases, the zombies accomplish the tasks assigned them—the letter of the law has been obeyed—but the ultimate results are always contrary to those of the zombie's would-be commander.)

Pirates, as you might imagine, are not generally known for their proclivity for obeying instructions, contracts, and laws. People who decide on a career in piracy are usually trying to get as far away as possible from places with rules that can bind them. As we've covered, a pirate flag itself is the very symbol for "I'm not playing by your rules." Also, pirates are notorious double-crossers and liars. They famously reverse their positions whenever it's to their advantage to do so. A European lawyer understands a contract to be a serious agreement with the power to bind someone forever, but for a pirate it is seen more as a vague mutual understanding governing the time between now and when the contract becomes in the slightest way inconvenient.

In summation, if a zombie is a bad employee, and a pirate is a bad employee, then zombie pirates are going to be **very bad employees.** And yet, dollars to doubloons, some high-ranking official at a European court is eventually going to start having thoughts along the lines of: "Hey . . . you know that one ship of zombie pirates that's been kicking everyone's ass—including ours—out there in the Caribbean all this time? What if—somehow, some way—they worked for us and they only kicked the asses of navies and merchant ships that were, you know, **not ours**?" This idea will appeal so greatly to the admiralties involved that they will in all likelihood decide it's at least worth trying (the potential benefits outweighing the cost of having a few emissaries eaten).

Pirates (or any other nautical mercenary types) who have to fight on one side of an international conflict are called "privateers." The idea is usually that the privateers agree not to attack merchant or army vessels of the nation commissioning them as privateers—say Spain—and are given free reign to attack vessels of other countries—say, France, Portugal, and Great Britain. In exchange for this, the pirates-cum-privateers are typically pardoned for any previous offenses committed against Spanish ships, the Spanish navy no longer attacks them on sight, and their pirate ship would be welcome to dock in Spanish-controlled ports. Spain benefits by increasing the number of pirate attacks against its enemies while eliminating pirate attacks against vessels flying the Spanish flag.

At least, that's how it's *supposed* to work. . . . With zombie pirates, things aren't going to go as the Europeans plan. (Mainstream privateering is **not** permitted under the Code of Zombie Piracy.)

When the representatives from Spain (or France, or Great Britain, or Portugal) arrive in a skiff flying a white flag—their delegation no doubt trembling in their doublets at the sight of your flesh-eating zombie crew—a number of options present themselves. You can:

- **Just eat them right away.** There's no need for your response to be as nuanced or eloquent as the pitch the Europeans are likely to make. You can simply answer their entreaty for a "mutual armistice" by creating "bloody armlessness" as your zombie crew rips them asunder. (The really amusing thing is that the Europeans will probably try again at least a couple more times. This is the only situation in which your zombie crew can expect a meal delivered directly to them, so you might as well let them enjoy it.)
- **Meet with them, but be open about your reluctance to work as privateers.** (Though why you wouldn't also eat them is frankly beyond me.) If you don't want to be bothered with entreaties to work as a privateer in the future, then doing this will get the message out.

- **Agree to serve as zombie pirate privateers in the employ of a European nation . . . but then, you know, don't.** This is the most fun to do if you have a particular prejudice against a certain European nationality. (They're all pretty annoying, if you ask me, but if there's one you've really got it in for, then this is the time to go for it!) Revenge is a dish best served out of the base of your enemy's skull. If there's a country you really hate, draw up a privateering agreement with them just so that you can break it. They will be delighted when you agree to take their side and devastated when they realize it has all been a ruse. You will be hurting their feelings—as opposed to just hurting them physically when your crew sacks their ship and eats them alive. It's a whole new world of pain you can inflict. Use it wisely.

- **Agree—secretly—to serve as zombie pirate privateers with all nations simultaneously.** If you like using subterfuge—and who doesn't?—then this is probably the most fun option of all. There's nothing keeping you from answering in the affirmative to the representatives of **all** the warring nations that come calling. The results of striking such agreements will be advantageous to you in a number of ways. Vessels that you do attack will not be expecting it, so surprise will always be yours. Further, if you attack your prey in an isolated piece of ocean (there are many) and scuttle the craft after your crew has picked it clean, then the ultimate fate of the vessel will remain a mystery to the sovereign nation. The European powers will have to intuit that you have broken your privateering agreement when their ships start to mysteriously go missing.

Conspicuously absent from the above options is the option of agreeing to work as a privateer for one nation **and then actually doing it.** This is because such an agreement is a very one-sided deal that is very bad for pirates and strictly forbidden under the Code. European nations ask privateers to take on all the danger of fighting in a war, with none of the benefits afforded enlisted men. For example, when a navy crew finds itself on the losing side of a sea battle, the sailors can expect to be taken as prisoners and held in accordance with international military law. Pirates (even if they claim to be working as privateers) will almost certainly be sentenced to hang. Zombie pirates have it even worse and can expect a musket ball through the brain without so much as a trial or tribunal. (The executioners will also probably call them names like "Stinking dirty pirate zombie bastards," which is just **so** unnecessary.)

European navies also supply their full-time navy sailors with supplies, food, the latest military intelligence, and a bevy of other helpful gifts. Freelancing privateers can expect nothing in the way of support from the nation they are serving.

"Oh, but wait," comes the objection from some pompous European naval officer (doubtless wearing some kind of ridiculous uniform with a bunch of stupid epaulets on his shoulder instead of a cool talking parrot). "You pirates get to keep all the treasure—and, erm, eat all the people—you plunder from the ships you attack. Regular enlisted navy men don't get to do **that**."

To which, any sensible zombie pirate must respond: "That's not an added inducement because **we were already doing that anyway!** Next you'll be telling us that if we become privateers you'll let us wear eye patches and tricorne hats and eat people's brains. It's, like, sorry, bub. We were doing that before."

(Zombie)
Pirate Ports

In popular culture, the notion exists of a "pirate port" in which sea-roving pirate ships can come and go as they please. In these theoretical ports, pirates can expect a friendly welcome from a populace with virtue flexible enough to ignore what they do for a living. At this port they can sell stolen goods, provision their ships, and enjoy all the accommodations entitled to any other wealthy, successful sailor.

Regrettably, it must be reported that these pirate ports are largely fictional, existing only insomuch as certain ports friendly to one nation would welcome privateers fighting its enemies, and even ports of flexible virtue do not flex so far as to welcome the undead ashore.

So what, then, is a zombie pirate captain—perhaps in need of only rest, barter, and an evening's diversion—to do?

The best option is probably disguise. Both zombies and pirates have long histories with this concept (though pirates probably ascribe more intentionality to the act of going incognito).

Zombies never employ deception on purpose; the idea does not occur to them. However, many freshly reanimated zombies are frequently mistaken for living humans. Even decomposing zombies can be mistaken for stunned or sickly humans when viewed from a great distance.

Pirates *regularly* employ deception in the course of their work. Pirates may fly the flag of any convenient nation in order to avoid encounters with hostile navies. They may don costumes and pose as traders or travelers. Some pirates use these tactics to ensnare unsuspecting prey, approaching a merchant ship under the flag

---

ZOMBIE TIP
Avoid the "Pirate Bay"

Despite what a bunch of Swedish copyright infringers might choose to do 300 years in the future, *actual* pirate bays are not fun places to hang out and exchange stolen movies. They are dangerous places to get stabbed and shot. (If you land in a pirate bay, your zombies will just try to eat all the pirates, and that's not going to lead anywhere good.)

of a friendly nation and only at the last moment hoisting their pirate flag and opening the gun ports.

If you're just looking for a little R&R, then you need to think only of how disguising your person can result in the ability to move freely on land.

A good disguise is important for your personal security. As a successful pirate captain, you are going to have enemies across the Caribbean and there will be rewards for your capture. At the helm of your ship, surrounded by terrifying zombies with daggers in their teeth, you are virtually invincible. Sneaking into Port-au-Prince under cover of darkness, you are extremely vulnerable. If people wanted to kill or capture you (and a lot of them do), then this would be the best possible time to do it.

Suffice to say, this calls for more than a putty nose and a fake beard.

The zombie pirate captain who truly wishes to travel incognito must aspire to craft a separate persona entirely. The more elaborate and detailed, the more likely it is to succeed.

Being a successful zombie pirate is a strange kind of fame. Many people know *of* you, but almost no one could pick you out of a lineup or describe your physical features.

You are not in the habit of sparing those you capture at sea, and dead men—and zombies—tell no tales. (Okay, maybe the *highest*-functioning zombie can "tell" something approaching a tale, but nine times out of ten it's just going to be a rambling narrative with a really heavy-handed message about how eating brains is awesome.) Because of this, concealing your distinguishing features is **not** your number-one priority when going ashore incognito. What is important is being able to present yourself, very convincingly, as someone other than who you actually are.

The biggest mistake you can make is just to walk into Port-au-Prince as a "mysterious stranger." You'll start throwing around gold—specific gold, that people will remember as having been plundered by "that zombie pirate" just a few weeks ago. Then somebody runs into the bar and announces he's seen the zombie pirate ship anchored off the coast, but no captain seemed to be aboard. Then the music suddenly stops and everybody looks over at you. Then at the Wanted poster the British government just put up advertising "A payement of not less than 3,000 goldene doubloonf for the heade of the nefariouf zombie pyrate." Then back at you.

When going incognito, you must present yourself in such a fashion that even if word reaches town that a zombie pirate captain is about, you will not be on a short list of possible candidates. Sometimes, the best way to do this is by going in the opposite direction, so to speak. Don't just be "a law-abiding citizen" or "a captain of some sort, but definitely not a zombie pirate." Be something so extremely opposite from what you actually are as to make all suspicion against you risible. Suggested personas include:

- **A pirate hunter,** fresh from the Carolina coast. You love to hunt down those rotten, evil pirates, and have heard that the Caribbean is just the place to do it. (This persona makes it easy to hang out with other sailors and "talk shop" without seeming to have a suspiciously high level of knowledge of maritime affairs.)

- **A wealthy shipping magnate** who is constantly plagued by the pirates who attack his valuable shipments of goods from the New World. (This persona is great if you want to throw around a lot of money while you're in town. Again, just make sure you use coins that didn't just go missing, or someone might notice.)

- **A European religious official,** like a monk or priest. Obviously, this persona will be scandalized by the very notion of zombies and voodoo, and will throw around phrases like "cleanse the unwashed heathens" and "destroy the obscene sacrilege that is an abomination to the Lord" and stuff. (This is the best persona to use when you just want to be left alone—maybe to go for a walk or get some errands done, stuff like that. Nobody ever suspects a European religious official of being "down" with the undead.)

If you like, you can use these as a jumping-off point and design your own. The key is to select a character that will allow you to move about freely and do what you came into port to do. Let's face it, your itinerary for the day may include things like selling stolen goods, drinking and gambling and womanizing, cavorting with pirates and sailors, and visiting voodoo priests and graveyards. The key is finding a way to weave qualities and traits into your character's backstory that make all of these activities plausible for you.

Also, be sure to be unpredictable. Change your character from time to time as needed. Don't always show up in the same port on the first of each month. People will start expecting you. Then they'll start asking questions about who you are and where you're from. You want to remain an outsider. A mystery.

Brine and Punishment

Nautical law and order has always been maintained by a ruthless enforcement of rules and regulations. Punishments aboard ships are nearly medieval in their severity. Pirates who disobey their captains, hoard treasure, or show cowardice in battle can be flogged, keelhauled, whipped, branded, marooned, or even executed. These measures are usually severe enough to keep even a group of professional murderers in line and working as a team.

How do you punish a zombie? How do you keep a zombie in line? How do you make a zombie behave? They sound like setups for unfunny jokes, but there's no comedy here. Just a pain in your ass. Disobedient zombie pirates can be a serious problem.

As near as anybody can tell, zombies are immune to physical pain. (That, or zombies are in a constant state of pain, and only eating brains can alleviate it.) Also, they have no sense of shame—as evinced by their frequent nudity—and so branding them traitors has very little effect.

All zombies want is brains. All zombies care about is getting to where brains are. Even the highest-functioning zombies will only perform tasks if they understand that these tasks are somehow connected to making brains happen. Any management of zombies, then, must arise from this single truth.

Zombie pirates are going to have discipline issues, but they're going to be different discipline issues from the ones you face with traditional pirates. Here are the major undead disciplinary failings, along with their proper remedies.

False-Positives for Brains: In truth, this is the failing for which disobedient zombie pirates can be most readily forgiven. Zombies are easily confused, and many things can appear brainlike in the heat of battle. Shadows that look vaguely humanoid can distract or startle a zombie. Tropical fruits and melons can, at a distance, create a false positive for human heads. Realistic masthead figures can grab a zombie's attention. As word of your zombie pirate crew spreads across the Caribbean, you may even find your foes *intentionally attempting to distract your zombies* with animal brains and so forth. Zombies must be coached to seek only the brains inside the living heads of your enemies. (To be fair, no zombie is *trying* to make this mistake. There is no advantage to a zombie when he momentarily mistakes a mannequin or a watermelon for an appropriate target.) In the case of this offense, a zombie's punishment should merely involve correction.

Militarily Negligent Decrepitude: We all know zombies are gross and rotting and falling apart, right? Sure. That's one of the things that makes them awesome. Human foes fear fighting disgusting, moldering zombies, and there can be advantages to zombie traits like overpowering odor, oleaginous slipperiness, and the fact that they can get an arm stuck in something and just let it fall off and keep advancing. However, some zombies have a *way* of coming apart that can endanger the zombies around them, and even the very success of your sea engagements. For example, zombies that are constantly leaking putrefaction ooze can cause other zombies to slip on the ooze and fall overboard. Zombies who are bloated and filled with gases from decaying in the hot Caribbean sun can unexpectedly explode (and take out other zombies adjacent to them). Zombies with pitchfork spikes or sharp shrapnel protruding

from their bodies—although totally amusing to behold—
may impale other zombies. If zombies in your pirate crew
have allowed themselves to approach this state in which
they are physically dangerous to their fellow zombie
pirates, then the first "punishment" should be surgery to
drain dangerous oozes and explosive gases and remove
spiky protrusions. If these surgeries are not successful
(or are too dangerous to attempt), you have no choice but
to throw the offending zombies overboard (or, if you're
feeling ambitious, to launch them with catapults onto the
decks of your enemies).

Ignoring the Order of Battle Play: When you're attacking
a European navy ship deck to deck, most of your zombie
pirates will automatically do what they should. They will
attack the nearest living human as viciously as possible and
attempt to eat his or her brains. Yet now and then, you may
find certain zombies with defects that steer them away from
this proper course of action. Certain zombies have been
known to attack recently dead humans who are no longer
combatants, or to stand around moaning while other zombies
are doing the fighting. While it has already been remarked
that certain zombies can be more skilled at certain tasks,
zombies who fail to keep pushing forward and attacking
humans require immediate correction. The "penalty" for
these disobedient zombies should be to be positioned in
situations where their failure to advance will not matter.

This should include places where you expect your enemies to concentrate their fire.

Attacking Ransomed Prisoners or Other Valuable Civilians: No! Bad zombie! I mean, what the hell, right? You go to all the trouble to kidnap the daughter of the Finance Minister of Tortuga, and just when you're thinking about how many pieces of eight she's worth to you (and how hot she looks in that crazy bustier thing she's wearing), you look up and see she's just been eaten by a zombie who couldn't wait until your next battle to get some brains. This situation is financially *and* sexually frustrating, and nobody would blame you for putting a lead ball in that zombie's brain right then and there. Instant destruction is an acceptable punishment for such an offense, but may also wish to punish such insatiably obstreperous zombies with "banishment." In its best form, this is accomplished when you encounter an enemy to whom you can present this zombie as a "gift." Then it's *his* problem.

Every pirate captain needs to mete out punishment to his or her crew now and then, and zombie pirate captains are no exception. If you strike the right balance between magnanimity and stern correction, your ship will run efficiently, and your zombies will respect you for it. (As much as zombies can be said to respect anything, that is.)

(Un)dead Man's Chest

Treasure. It's what there is in the Caribbean. It's why you're here.

In the sense that pirates use the term, "treasure" refers to small physical objects with greatly concentrated monetary value. When pirates capture a ship, only a small fraction of the many items aboard will actually qualify as the kind of treasure a pirate is looking for. These qualifying items include gold and silver coins (or anything made from gold and silver, really), money and notes of legal tender, historical artifacts, jewelry, and precious stones (the smaller and more valuable, the better). When looting a ship, pirates will stuff every pocket with this high-value-concentration treasure.

Other captured items do not qualify as "pirate treasure"—strictly speaking—because they aren't concentrated wealth that's easily transportable. For example, a merchant ship may be full of rum, cotton, sugarcane, or some similar commodity of value. Although pirates might plunder a little rum for personal use, these commodities do not constitute "pirate treasure," because only **a whole lot of it** is really valuable. Pirates—and **especially** zombie pirate captains—don't have room for a whole lot of anything on their ships, so they have to be very selective. Also, finding a fence who wants a cargo hold full of cotton is often more trouble than it's worth. So while a vessel laden with "20 tonnes of flax from the Newe Worlde" may technically be transporting "a cargo of great value," it is also useless to a pirate, who hasn't the room to transport any captured flax or a friendly port in which to sell it. Livestock—though less frequently transported—is another good example. Pirates may take some animals for their own eating, but transporting a herd of something for sale is just not in the cards.

ZOMBIE TIP
Bejeweled . . .

Some people incorrectly associate pirates with fops or dandies because of the way they often wear jewelry. Really, though, wearing captured jewels is just another way to transport them. If you see a pirate walking around in earrings and a tiara, it's probably just because his pockets are already full and he has no place else to put them.

Thus, when pirates overtake a wealthy merchant ship, their first move is **not** to storm into the hold and see what's being transported. Rather, they line up and systematically rob the merchants onboard of their money and personal possessions. After this, they check to see if the ship has any sort of strongbox where the travelers might be holding any other highly concentrated and easily transportable wealth. It is only after the upper decks have been picked clean of anything valuable and shiny that the pirates bother to see what's "down below." On occasion they do get crazy lucky, and a ship is carrying gold bars or something, but most frequently it's just a bunch of cargo that pirates don't have the space for.

In rare cases, captured items can be hard to classify, and the pirate can be forced to make a tough call. For example, the deed to a house in London is of little immediate value to a pirate who is here in the Caribbean. However, he may be able to sell it to someone bound for England, or even to another pirate looking to retire somewhere rainy and overcast. An exotic animal plundered from a vessel of naturalists returning from the Galapagos may be of little immediate value (and probably looks too weird to try to eat), but the right collector might be willing to pay a hefty fee for an exotic bird or lizard of questionable provenance.

Back aboard their ship, pirates fixate like crows on the shiny baubles they have captured in combat. Spending days and days at sea gives you plenty of time to examine, order, polish, and catalog your jewels, coins, and other valuables. As their treasure accumulates, pirates tend to store it in boxes and chests of increasing size. Finally, it is possible for a pirate to accumulate so much plundered wealth that it no longer becomes advisable to keep it aboard ship. When this happens, it is a serious problem. The pirate's chest can be robbed (as indeed, many are—usually by the pirate's own shipmates). It can be tossed overboard in rough seas or lost forever if the ship were to sink. If arrested, the pirate's treasure will be seized by the authorities, who will (shudder) try to return it to its rightful original owners.

What to do? Depositing such obviously ill-gotten wealth at a financial institution will arouse too much suspicion. In fact, entrusting one's looted lucre to any landlubber is a risky proposition. If there were only some way treasure could be safe on land—safe from other pirates *and* from sinking into the sea—but in such a way that nobody knows about it . . .

Hence, the great tradition of buried treasure.

Burying treasure is a cerebral feat. It's all about controlling knowledge and information—limiting it, to be precise. One of the only sure means of ensuring the safety of plundered valuables is to limit the number of people who know where the valuables are. The fewer the better. (Optimally, only the owner of the treasure will have any inkling as to its whereabouts.)

Burying a treasure chest on a remote and deserted island is by far the most popular way of overcoming this "limitation." However, it is not the only way. Many famous pirates have "buried" treasure simply by hiding it. Treasure can be tied to an anchor and sunk in shark-infested waters. It can be secured deep inside a cave or high on a mountain. Any approach is acceptable as long as it limits the number of people who know where to find your treasure.

As a zombie pirate captain, you can expect to accumulate treasure rather quickly. You can also expect to run out of space for it sooner rather than later. (Your ship's hold is full of zombies, zombies, and more zombies, remember?) Safely securing your hard-stolen money and valuables is going to be something you do with considerable frequency.

Say you're ready to bury some treasure. The first question is "Where?" Options abound in the great big Caribbean. But so do dangers. Uninhabited-looking islands can turn out to be home to native peoples who will be quick to notice a great big pile of disturbed earth. Erosion can wash away layers of sand—sometimes several inches a year—leaving a treasure chest that was once buried four feet deep just a few years ago exposed for all the world to see. And—worst of all—remote caves and caverns can turn out to have already been used **by another pirate.** (And you'd better hope he's not there at the time, because then it just degenerates into a "two hermit crabs fighting over the same shell"-type scenario, which nobody wants.)

To avoid these and other negative results, the Code of Zombie Piracy prescribes the following guidelines when burying treasure:

- Pick an island. (Burying something on the mainland would be cunningly counterintuitive, but the increased risk of someone stumbling onto the site where you've buried your treasure makes it a bad bet.)
- Pick a place on the island that is not only isolated but also has a reputation as being haunted. Then, make it be **actually haunted** by leaving a bunch of zombies there. (Picking a location without a sinister reputation is bad. The presence of the zombies will arouse curiosity instead of dread.)
- Pick a small island, **but not one that's comically tiny.** People sailing by shouldn't wonder: "Hey, why does that ten feet by thirty feet island have twelve zombies on it? I wonder how they got there. . . Maybe we should stop and take a look."

- Setting booby traps around your buried treasure is fine, but you must employ booby traps **that don't appear to be booby traps.** When visitors land on a remote island (to search for gold, catalog indigenous species, dump a body, etc.), the presence of booby traps is going to make them curious. If explorers encounter massive pits filled with wooden spikes, tripwires that launch spring-loaded arrows, and nets that fall from the ceilings of caves, they're going to wonder what was so darn important that somebody bothered to leave all these traps lying in wait. Obvious booby traps will turn travelers into treasure hunters, and treasure hunters into *determined* treasure hunters, and you don't want that. Instead, use only booby traps with consequences and effects that appear to be "accidents." Position boulders that will trigger dangerous rockslides. Hew false steps (designed to give way) in precarious mountain paths. Position alligators in unexpected places. Only by camouflaging your traps as natural accidents will you ensure that they actually do encourage people to avoid the place where your treasure is hidden.

- Make plenty of treasure maps **to places where your treasure is not.** Seriously, you're a smart, capable guy/gal, right? You've captained a ship of zombie pirates successfully enough to have more treasure than you know what to do with. Are you seriously telling me that you can't remember where you left **one** thing? (One **very**

important thing?) A good zombie pirate captain can remember where his or her loot is stashed, and should only draw up treasure maps for the purpose of throwing off would-be thieves. (If you like, you can make it a prank and draw maps to locations where you've buried trunks of zombies that will spring up when the "treasure chest" is opened and consume any would-be treasure hunters.)

- Finally, **don't tell anybody** where you buried the treasure. This one sounds obvious, but you'd be surprised how many pirate captains go blabbing about their booty after one too many rum smoothies. Luckily, you're going to be spending most of your time around zombies, who are far more interested in brains than treasure. Anything you say onboard your ship will fall on ears that are—for all practical purposes—deaf. Just make sure that when you pull into port you don't forget yourself and spill the beans. (Also, being a zombie pirate captain is not about boasting. If you need to talk about all the treasure you've buried to feel like a big man, then, dude, you're in the wrong business.)

Now that we've covered the steps necessary to successfully hiding your own plundered treasure, let's explore another important part of the Code of Zombie Piracy: **taking the treasure of others.**

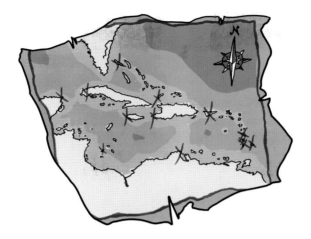

As a zombie pirate captain who sails the high seas preying upon widows and orphans (and stupid European navies), you ought to have no compunction about preying upon other pirates when the regrettable situation arises. While the Pirate Code might frown upon pirates stealing from other pirates, the Zombie Pirate Code actively encourages it (making it nearly compulsory). And while ship-to-ship conflicts with your non-undead counterparts are not recommended, if you find a pirate's treasure map that appears to be reliable, then it's **game fucking on!**

Just as you—if you're wise—will take great pains to draw up false treasure maps to mislead those that would steal your own plundered goods, so do other pirate captains construct phony directions to their treasure to throw treasure hunters off the scent. Thus, when you do chance to obtain a map to another pirate's treasure, the first step in the process should be verifying its authenticity. Begin by asking yourself these questions:

- **How difficult was it to find this map?** If the map was stolen from a conspicuous nightstand in a pirate's private quarters—and tied with a ribbon lettered to read: "Secret Pirate Treasure Map! DO NOT STEAL!"—then it is probably a dummy. If, however, the map you possess was found locked in a secret strongbox, concealed behind a false wall, or tattooed on the scalp of a fierce pirate (who took ten of your best zombies to kill) then you may have the real thing.

- **How detailed is this map?** Typically, forgers make things a bit too detailed. That's right, I'm saying that the *more* detailed a treasure map is, the *less* likely it is to be authentic. In most cases, a pirate who buries his treasure only draws a map order to remind **himself** of where he put it. No pirate intends to draw up an easy-to-read guide that *anyone* can use to find his treasure. (Remember: His purpose is to keep it secret and safe from **everyone except himself.**) If your map is plain and cryptic, you may be on a better track. Esoteric descriptions of places and things are also a reliable indicator of authenticity. (If an island is labeled "that one place that had the red trees" and a bay is named "that spot where Olaf swore he saw a mermaid," you're probably on to something good.)

- **Does the map have riddles, puzzles, and clues that require knowledge of history and world events in order to solve?** If so, it is definitely a forgery—and probably not even made by a real pirate. Most practitioners of the piratical arts have more important things to do with their time than accrue a working knowledge of anagrams or ciphers. (Heck, most pirates would probably have trouble writing their own names.) Likewise, actual puzzle-makers might enjoy fantasizing about using their skills to craft a delightfully cunning treasure map, but they tend to be weakling landlubbers with desk jobs who will never accrue any treasure worth making a map to.

- **Who benefits from your following this map?** If the answer is: "Nobody except you," then congratulations—you might have an actual treasure map. However, if there are entities in the area that would, say, derive an advantage from sending you on a wild-goose chase after false treasure, you're going to want to think long and hard before jaunting off to where the map points. If you've been fighting the local colonial navies, plundering the shit out of merchant ships with your awesome zombie crew, and leaving no spoils in the area for the other pirates (who may be facing the prospect of getting day jobs or something equally revolting), then your list of enemies is probably a long one. After years of trying to hunt you down, they've probably realized you're too much of a badass to kill or sink. Sending you away on a months-long search for treasure might be their best bet. So if you take a suspiciously easy-to-capture merchant vessel and find aboard a map to a giant mother lode of treasure that will require you to travel to the other side of the globe to find, consider it carefully before you set sail.

The above list is not designed to dissuade you from pursuing buried treasure. Rather, it is intended to help you streamline the process. (You should never have to face that horrible moment where you stop to wipe your brow and lean on your shovel as you declaim in frustration: "What gives? We dug up the whole island, and still nothing!" And then you slowly realize: Maybe we aren't finding any treasure because **this is not a real treasure map.**)

Finding actual buried treasure is totally excellent, and a real time-saver to boot. It can take months of plundering to amass the concentrated wealth found in one treasure chest (and it all comes in an easy-to-carry case). After a while, you should expect to get a feel for the maps showing where actual treasure is buried. Happy hunting!

Caribbean, Idle

Downtime. You knew it was going to be a part of this gig.

Sometimes weather, politics, or just the time of year will reduce the number of merchant ships upon which you can prey. European navies may not be around to "play with" as they get called back to Europe to reload, refit, or to participate in battles on the other side of the Atlantic. Fellow pirates who are tired of competing with you (and/or being attacked by you) can shove off up the coast to attack ships in the American colonies.

It is a commandment of the Code of Zombie Piracy that you learn to emulate the zombies in your crew during

these "downtimes" and wait patiently for things to pick up. Attacking something other than ships (like towns or forts) just because no ships are around or leaving the Caribbean entirely and looking for prey elsewhere are not permitted actions.

Like a zombie—who has infinite patience—a zombie pirate captain must show self-control and learn to tolerate the delays that will inevitably occur. Cultivating a zombie-like ability to stay aboard ship for days and days and days with no new stimulus is an important part of a zombie pirate captain's effectiveness.

Where you must face the potential isolation that goes with being on a ship with a bunch of dead guys (who can hardly talk, much less recommend books or share juicy gossip), other pirate crews face the opposite problem. The typical pirate ship—when it is not actively attacking another vessel—naturally tends toward becoming something like a floating casino, with the captain forced to expend all his energies to muster the discipline to keep this from happening. Left to their own, typical pirates will almost instantly revert to drinking, gambling, and general carrying-on. A leading cause of death among pirates is injuries resulting from alcohol-related accidents, such as sustaining a fatal wound during a drunken brawl with shipmates.

What I'm saying here is thank your lucky stars that you have a crew of undead zombies aboard your ship. In *their* idle moments, zombie pirates will usually just stand around and moan. While they do sometimes kill one another, this is a rare occurrence and always an accident. (Zombie pirates can bump into one another, sending one or both overboard, or accidentally impale their heads on weapons.) Because zombies are in it for the brains

> **ZOMBIE TIP**
> **Call me "Zombie" . . .**
>
> They say that the moral of *Moby-Dick* is that it doesn't make sense to get angry at acts of nature. It does, however, make sense to get angry at zombie pirates, especially if they've murdered your crew, sacked your ship, and left you marooned on a boring island somewhere. Expect a lot of people to be angry with you, I guess is what I'm saying.

(as opposed to for the money), they will have nothing worth gambling for or fighting over. (Do make sure they get enough brains on a regular basis, though, or you're going to have some cranky zombies.)

Ever wonder why you have such an easy time defeating other pirate crews? Yes, yes, your crew is a bunch of zombies who can only be killed by severing their heads or destroying their brains. But also consider that the human pirates are going to be suffering from powerful hangovers, distracting gambling addictions, and personal grudges against other pirates serving on their own crew.

Zombies are always going to be as reliable as zombies. There is no "zombie on a good day." Zombies are always at their maximum level of effectiveness.

As you cruise the Caribbean looking for plunder, understand that the "silence of the zombies" aboard your ship is also the sweet sound of success. You are the envy of pirate captains everywhere who must contend with hangovers and hurt feelings among their men.

Full Zombie Captaincy: The Ultimate Level of Devotion

Up to this point, we have explored the benefits (and, yes, drawbacks) of commanding a pirate crew of zombies. Yet it has thus far been presumed that you, the reader, would, as pirate captain, choose to remain human. What about captains who seek to make the ultimate dedication to their art? Is it possible—they might ask—to *be* a zombie even as one commands a crew of them?

A difficult question, yes, but there does seem to be evidence that a few particularly enterprising pirate captains have made the transition to "full zombie." The great Blackbeard himself is a likely candidate for this. (Whether this was a good move or a lousy one is the subject of some debate.) As many know, at the outset of his career in piracy, Blackbeard engaged in many unzombie-like activities including eating food, smoking hashish, and enjoying sexual intercourse with women. Yet toward the end of his life, Blackbeard appears to have become **very** like a zombie. His bloodthirstiness was unchallenged. His predilection for murder and violence—even, for no reason, against members of his own crew—became legendary. Blackbeard seemed to pursue murder for its own sake. While some have argued that this indiscriminate murderousness was a calculated strategy on Blackbeard's part to instill fear in his enemies, it must also be noted that a ravenous appetite for violence is also consistent with his being a zombie.

Of course, the strongest argument for Blackbeard's membership in the legion of the walking dead is the manner in which he met his own death (or, perhaps, "death"). The authorities who had pursued the infamous pirate for so long only met with success when they employed tactics consistent with hunting zombies, not pirates.

When Lieutenant Robert Maynard of the British Navy sailed from Virginia to attack Blackbeard off the coast of North Carolina, he knew that no quarter would be asked or granted. Blackbeard seemed to have become incapable of taking prisoners and simply fought and fought until everyone was dead. Like a zombie, Blackbeard had no sense of the conventions of war or of surrender. Maynard also brought two ships to attack Blackbeard's single vessel (perhaps mindful that victory is nearly impossible when zombies have greater numbers). When the ships met and the fighting started, Blackbeard boarded Maynard's ship. Even though he was outnumbered, Blackbeard could only attack. Like a zombie, his lone setting was "Kill all humans."

Most tellingly, during the course of the bloody sword- and pistol-fighting that ensued, Blackbeard is recorded as having sustained

> **ZOMBIE TIP**
> Sea of Gory . . .
>
> Whilst some maritime warriors fight to bring "glory" to a particular ethos, nation, or religious deity, zombies enjoy the fight at sea for the simple purpose of eating people's brains. For a zombie, there is nothing higher (or lower) than defeating one's enemies and gorging upon the organs they used to think with.

not fewer than twenty sword wounds, and between five and twenty pistol wounds (depending on the version of the story), before expiring. (If that's not a zombie's battle-field resilience, I don't know what is.) To be sure he was dead, Maynard **cut Blackbeard's head from its body** and mounted it on the bowsprit of one of his ships.

So, if Blackbeard **was** a zombie, was that fact the secret of his success? It is a difficult question.

Certainly, facing a crew of snarling, teeth-gnashing zombies is certainly a terrifying prospect for any merchant ship or navy vessel—and seeing a ship of zombies **also captained**

by a zombie would only drive the terror of the humans involved to the nth degree—but going "full zombie" can also have several drawbacks for pirate captains. Blackbeard, for example, had amassed enough plunder and riches to retire to his own private island (where nobody was going to fuck with him—c'mon, he was Blackbeard). Yet it seemed not to sate him. He seemed to like fighting for its own sake, and so chose to engage Robert Maynard's force instead of sensibly fleeing the larger opponent.

Zombie captains hunger for only for brains and the close combat it takes to secure them. Zombie captains also have no "magic number" of brains they are trying to eat before being able to retire comfortably. They, like their crews, will kill and kill and kill until they themselves are destroyed. (Once you choose the "zombie option," there is no going back).

Other potential drawbacks of zombie captaincy include:

- An inability to focus on long-term piracy projects. (Whatever brains are closest becomes pretty much all-encompassing.)
- Illiteracy. (True, you weren't out there to brush up your Shakespeare or write the great Caribbean novel, but being able to read maps and compasses is pretty important if you're a pirate in the year 1700, tough guy.)
- Loss of ability to appreciate traditional pirate plunder (gold, women, rum, etc.).

- Your ability to command and inspire through articulate speech is replaced with the ability only to moan and gesture.

It's important as a zombie pirate captain—just as in any other field—to step back and look at the big picture. Take the time to remember *why* you're doing something. Maybe you became a zombie pirate captain to kick the asses of those stupid European navies who like pushing everybody around. That's great, but remember, zombies just attack whatever humans are nearest. Zombie pirate captains aren't able to discriminate between friends and foes. They're as likely to attack fellow pirates as they are the Spanish navy.

We all know that zombies are relentless, awesome killing machines. That's why you want to captain a crew of them. But think very carefully before going to see the voodoo shaman or taking that dirt nap in a haunted graveyard your-self. Zombie pirates need someone to get them crewing in the right direction and to focus their murderous energies on appropriate targets. They need, in short, someone with brains. Functioning brains. If you decide to forfeit that asset and join the zombies' dark parade of delighted slaughter, you may ultimately jeopardize the effectiveness of your crew, and you will certainly lose the ability to focus your efforts specifically upon those who have wronged you.

P-p-p-pirate
Ghosts?

Yes, pirate ghosts.

The Caribbean is a haunted, lawless place where indigenous spiritual practices meet ones imported from Europe
and Africa and meld together into a mélange that's liable to
confuse even the most coolheaded revenant.

Throughout your travels across the night-washed shores of
the Spanish Main, you are liable to encounter your share of
haunts and specters. If there was ever a place for a ghost to
hang out, it's the Caribbean at night. (What is the sea itself if
not a giant graveyard of ships and men? And the forts, cities,
and military outposts that dot the land have been the scenes

of enough carnage and inhumanity to inspire an army of malevolent spirits.) Let me be perfectly clear about this: In the Caribbean, **you will see ghosts.**

Believe it or not, as the captain of a pirate ship full of zombies, you will appear a receptive subject for pirate ghosts (and other ghosts) who are looking to communicate with the living. Pirate ghosts don't usually get anybody to talk to. European religious officials typically frown upon communication with the dead, and voodoo priests operate on a strictly fee-based system. A ghost who sees a dude commanding a ship full of undead zombies is a ghost who is going to get excited.

Most ghosts, however, you can be perfectly content to ignore. Ghosts in this category include "scary haunters" who attach themselves to abandoned caves and burned-out forts. (It's, like, it's just a stupid old fort. I wasn't even going there anyway, so why are you getting all moany about it?) Weeping/crying ghosts of jilted lovers and relatives lost at sea can also be ignored. (And *should* be; they're so annoying.) Sprites and balls of light that flitter

on and off in the night do not require your attention either (though they may prove useful when navigating in the dark). Ghostly bloodstains in the sand (or along rock walls) may likewise be ignored.

Humanoid apparitions, on the other hand, are worth investigation. Many human-seeming ghosts just want someone to chat with. Others still want to tell you about how they met their death unjustly, through some intricate betrayal that they of course want to enlist **you** to put right. (As if you've got all the time in the world to just fuck off and help ghosts whenever they ask!) But **sometimes** . . . just **sometimes** . . . ghosts will moan their way to your attention because they are the ghosts of former pirates who have something useful to tell you.

The big one here, obviously, is buried treasure. Many pirates who have buried their treasure lose their lives before they get a chance to dig it back up and enjoy it. Few things are more frustrating than this. Superior even to the anguish created by forfeiting the chance to enjoy one's treasure is the thought that it might be lost forever—sitting untouched in a sandbank (until some fat, sunburned tourist with a metal detector finds it three hundred years later).

Pirates are also arrogant, and they want their stories told. Their treasure is a way of doing this.

A pirate's treasure is more than just a chest full of gold and diamonds and jewelry. It's also a testament to his many successes over the years. Each piece is meaningful. Each piece tells a story. (*This* particular brooch was plucked from a beautiful maiden aboard a Dutch freighter. *That* diamond was harvested from the pocket of a famous Spanish diplomat. *These* gold coins were received in payment from the French for sinking a Portuguese warship.) A pirate's treasure chest is like his scrapbook. Memories from a lifetime of piracy are accumulated within. Thus, when a pirate dies an untimely death *with his treasure buried*, it is as though his story has died with him.

Pirate ghosts usually want their treasure found because it means their story will live on. You will be the pirate who dug up "Bluebeard's treasure" or so forth. The pirate ghost will get a little vicarious thrill and will see his exploits recalled to mind at least once more.

Thus, when you see a probable pirate ghost beckoning to you from a forgotten cove or hidden inlet, it is usually worth your time to investigate. Weigh anchor, go ashore, and attempt to address the pirate directly. What ensues will be a two-way audition. You want to see if this is really a useful pirate ghost, and (if it is) the pirate ghost will want to see that you are a pirate of some esteem and accomplishment, worthy of his treasure. If you're worried about your pirate sea cred, take some zombies with you as you go ashore. Make clear to the ghost that you're a **zombie** pirate captain, with all the added badassery that conveys.

Even with your zombies in tow, the pirate ghost may still require you to answer a riddle, demonstrate skill with a rapier, or any number of other proficiencies. Come prepared, or at least semi-sober.

If you successfully impress the pirate ghost, then you shouldn't have far to go. **His treasure is probably nearby.** The ghosts of slain pirates tend not to haunt not the spot in the middle of the ocean where the pirate met his watery fate, but the area where the pirate once buried his treasure. The treasure burial site is the most significant terrestrial place for a pirate, so this is logical.

When the pirate ghost leads you to the spot where his treasure is buried, he will disappear into thin air. Mark the spot where he vaporizes, because that's where you want to start digging. With any luck, a treasure will soon be yours, and a restless spirit will finally be put to sleep.

A notable variant of the pirate ghost may, from time to time, present itself in the form of the "ghost ship." These spectral barks are the malevolent spirits of **entire pirate crews** that have gone down to the briny deep together. Ghost ships are not generally dangerous (with one notable exception to be dealt with in a moment). Typically, ghost ships will not approach you. If you do choose to approach one of them, its denizens will most likely ask that you pass along messages to their friends and families, who are of course long dead. (Maybe you will get lucky, and one of the friends or family members will now be a zombie aboard your own ship, but this is a relatively minuscule possibility.) Ghost ships are just a floating dead letter office.

Only one ghost ship is actually dangerous: The *Flying Dutchman.* It is different from others because it is possessed by a malevolent spirit. Though many have theorized as to who the captain of the *Dutchman* might be—though Bernard Fokke, the Dutch merchant trader, is a common (if incorrect) guess—no crew has ever been seen aboard the *Dutchman.* This is because the ship is not a ship at all. It is a sentient ghost that wants to bring harm and ruin to seafarers. It is an ancient spirit that only assumes the shape of a ship for convenience. It is evil, and it is always in a bad mood.

The *Flying Dutchman* has been seen in oceans all around the world, and invariably described as a moldering sloop with ragged sails and an eerie glow about it. (It is usually seen at night, either just after sunset or directly before dawn.) It will **definitely** show up in the Caribbean from time to time.

The *Dutchman*'s threat is an indirect one. It will not attempt to attack you, and has no working guns or cannons. However, glimpsing the Dutchman is **very bad luck.**

Lookouts, who are usually the first to see it, routinely slip and fall from their crow's nests. Ship's crews are unnerved by its presence and experience all manner of unexpected misfortunes in the days following a sighting. Even the steeliest sea salts are not immune to the *Dutchman*'s spell. And ships' captains? Let's just say that they are especially susceptible to the powers of this spirit ship. A record of madness, suicide, and murder follows in the biographies of those sea captains who have seen the *Dutchman.*

Luckily, the effects of the *Dutchman* can be mitigated if you keep your head about you. Seeing the *Dutchman* is a bit like locking your keys inside your house. As you do it, you think to yourself: "Wait . . . did I just leave my keys insi—" Many sea captains who see the *Dutchman* have a "Wait . . . is that the *Flying Dutchman*? It couldn't be, could it? No. No way. But it sure looks . . . I mean, that glow and all . . . So wait . . . **Is** it . . . ?" response. Consequently, when they realize that it **is** the *Dutchman*—and they, you know, shouldn't be looking at it—they've already been eyeballing it for a good ten minutes (which is more than enough time for a curse to take hold).

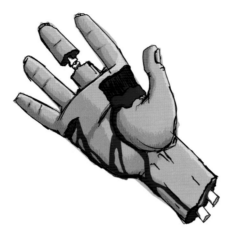

Experience has not shown, however, that there are any deleterious effects from fleeting glimpses of the *Dutchman*. Thus, a mindful zombie pirate captain has a good chance of avoiding its nefarious effects. Just remember the following:

- Whenever you see something glowing that shouldn't be glowing, look away immediately.
- If a ship on the horizon looks abandoned and about two hundred years old, look away immediately.
- If you see a ship with *Flying Dutchman* stenciled on its bow, for God's sake look away immediately.

After averting your eyes during a possible *Dutchman* sighting, you should order that a dinghy filled with your highest-functioning zombies (your seconds, carpenters, gunners, zombies who can still talk a little bit and take direction) sent to ascertain if in fact it is the *Dutchman* and not just a derelict boat laden with phosphorous. If your zombie expeditionary party does not return with an explanation for the ship—and/or they mysteriously begin to crumble into dust or burst into flames—then you may have the real thing on your hands. Whatever your current objective may be, forget it for the moment and give the order to sail away from the *Dutchman.* Then, go belowdecks and **do not emerge** until dawn. (You may also wish to blindfold yourself as an added precaution.)

Though they might seem overcautious, these procedures are the only proven way to avoid the effects of the *Dutchman.* While a night spent in the company of a bunch of zombie pirates in your ship's hold might not be your idea of an exciting evening, it is vastly preferable to risking contracting a horrible curse from a malignant, malevolent spirit ship.

An Ending Worthy of a Zombie Pirate

What does "success" look like for a zombie pirate?

For most, just not being captured or killed is enough to have made their careers "successful." Let's face it: Piracy is an incredibly dangerous job. Almost nobody gets out alive, and those who do seldom emerge unscathed (as wooden legs, eye patches, and long prison sentences evince). Even fame—that much desired and ephemeral mistress—is no protection against a grisly end. Many of the **most famous** pirates meet inglorious demises on the wrong end of cutlasses or swinging from the gallows. (If a pirate is executed, then his body—or just his head—is usually then put on public display as a warning to those who would consider a piratical career. Perhaps further "fame" is thus derived, but who wants *that*?)

Few pirate captains make it out of the profession alive. Fewer still manage to retire to a nice island somewhere with all of their loot. In a way, getting out of the "game" of piracy is a little like trying to get out of a crime syndicate. It's hard enough for someone at the top to do it, and almost impossible for a lower-level functionary. However, there are a few—just a few—tried-and-true precedents.

Realistic options for getting out of the game of piracy include:

Obtaining Clemency from a European Nation—Look, I'm not going to say I won't be a little disappointed if you choose this one, but lots of pirates do it. Not that it's easy. It does involve work. Like, let's say you've been a pirate in the Caribbean for years, preying on ships of every registry imaginable. You decide you want out, so you go to England and say: "You're at war with Spain, right? How about, for the next few years, I only attack Spanish ships. Then, after that, maybe you let me retire to England, and maybe I'm not a pirate anymore?" This is obviously close to privateering (which has already been considered and discouraged). And while some very successful pirates have taken this way out—Henry Morgan sank so many Spanish ships that he was knighted for it—you don't get a lot of respect at the "pirates' reunion" if you do.

Disappearing—Sailing off into the sunset can be a very practical choice for a pirate, yet history shows that few have managed it. It sounds easy enough, doesn't it? Just sail off to a part of the world where nobody knows you and start an awesome new life financed by *massive chests full of pirate treasure.* However, pirates are an odd breed. After a few rums or ales, they have difficulty not boasting of their daring illegal deeds back in the Caribbean. They can also have trouble fitting in with members of polite society after spending twenty years in an all-out festival of debauchery and crime. This option remains easier said than done.

Faking Your Own Death—This is obviously the best option for a pirate who wants to retire. European navies won't come looking for somebody they think is already dead, now will they? Other pirates with grudges against you will call off the hunt (assuming the hand of providence already smote you on their behalf). With "your" head sticking on a pike back at the capital—and a corresponding drop in the amount of overall piracy—there will be no question as to your fate. Except, really, you won't be dead at all. You'll have passed off an impostor as yourself, or have loaded your ship with gunpowder and sailed it right at the Spanish (the resulting explosion being something nobody could possibly survive . . . unless they weren't on the ship in the first place, which will be the case). As with disappearing, there is the danger of betraying yourself at a later date, but it seems that when pirates have invested the time and ingenuity required to successfully fake their own deaths, they're less likely to blab about it for no reason.

Pirates have it easy, at least when compared to zombies.

Those who would create, control, and lord over zombies almost always come to a bad end. Typical people in this category could include:

- Industrial magnates who create zombies with chemical byproducts.
- Power-mad dictators who seek to create an army of zombie supersoldiers.
- Discredited doctors who create zombies in medically unsanctioned experiments.
- Wizards using the black arts to staff their castles with zombie servants.

There are, frankly, no good endings for those who deal in zombies, just ones that are "less bad." Those who create and harness zombies—if they survive the process physically— often face financial ruin, social isolation, and other setbacks. Typical "less bad" endings include:

The Public Humiliation—When an uncaring industrialist's factory produces toxic waste that seeps into the ground and creates zombies, that industrialist is *usually* killed by the zombies, but not always. In some cases, they merely destroy his factory, wipe out his workforce, and somehow end up exposing his systematic neglect of EPA guidelines. Things come to a climax with the industrialist being chased through his own factory by a horde of zombies. He encounters well-armed survivors who offer to protect him, but only if he comes clean about his role in the sudden presence of the undead. Invariably, the industrialist falls to his knees and—between sobs of contrition—confesses his wrongdoing. The story usually ends with the zombie outbreak contained, but the industrialist, contrite as he may be, being lead away in handcuffs (or at least testifying before a Senate committee).

The Certified Insanity—Sometimes mad doctors and scientists who create zombies avoid the chair or the hangman's noose (or just the angry mob with pitchforks) by arguing that they are literally, legally "mad" and should be removed to an asylum—probably on a haunted island somewhere—for the remainder of their lives. (Again, I didn't say these were good options . . . just "less bad.")

The Zombification of the Zombifier—Quite a few voodoo shamans and witch doctors have met this end, usually at the hands of their personal enemies. It's a kind of poetic justice when a practitioner of voodoo—who has ruined the lives of others for many years by creating zombies—is finally captured and turned into a zombie himself, and not just any zombie. He can expect to spend eternity performing the most degrading and menial tasks his creators can think up. He'll be passed down in perpetuity from generation to generation, like an undead heirloom, until he finally crumbles into dust.

The Fitting Banishment—Some practitioners of the zombie arts desire to use the undead to create an empire in which they are an all-powerful center of attention. For these unfortunates, no ending is more stinging—and more likely to happen—than their banishment to anonymity on a remote island. The island invariably contains only the smoldering ruins of the destroyed empire they hoped to build on the backs of zombies. Whatever the exact specifics of the banishment, it is a fate worse than death. For a person who uses zombies to become powerful and connected, there is no greater living nightmare than to end his days powerless and alone.

Throughout your storied career as a zombie pirate captain, **you've used zombies to further your own ends.** There's no getting around it. You've created zombies (or hired others to do so) whenever you saw fit. You've built an empire of piracy on their undead backs. You've made a career of putting zombies into dangerous situations and then sitting back and benefiting from their hard work.

You are culpable. You are an exploiter of zombies.

However, your salvation is not impossible. Because of the unique forces at play in the combination of zombies and piracy, you can find unique ways of extricating yourself from a life of piracy even as you physically extricate yourself from a pirate crew of zombies. Let's look at what you need to do and how to get it done.

Several immediate problems are facing you:

- Because of your status as their captain/shaman/witch-doctor, many of your higher-functioning zombies will be tempted to follow you, even when you no longer wish them to. You need to find a way to wrap up these loose zombie ends before retiring.
- "What the fuck happened to you?" That's what merchants, colonial governors, other pirates—hell,

basically everyone in the Caribbean is going to be asking once you disappear. You're going to have to give an accounting for your new whereabouts, be it real or manufactured.

- You've accumulated a lot of treasure. If you've done things right, it's buried all over the place. If you want to enjoy wealth in your sunset years, you're going to have to figure out a suitable ruse that will allow you to collect this treasure while not revealing your past as a zombie pirate.

- "Who are you?" If you're not a zombie pirate captain anymore, then what will your new persona be? You're going to have to pick an identity—like you do when you go ashore incognito—and be willing to keep up the charade for the rest of your days (which, if you drink like a pirate, might not be all that long).

They might seem daunting, but if you approach these problems sensibly and systematically, it shouldn't be long before you are living free and easy (with a brand-new name and a bank account that boggles the mind).

To start with, there is you, and there is your nautical army of zombies. The easiest way to divest yourself of the latter is to make an assault on a merchant vessel, strand your zombies on it, and sink it. Attack the vessel as you normally would, but after your boats are joined and your zombies have spilled onto the merchant vessel's decks, cut the grappling lines that bind your ships, leaving as many of your zombies as possible still fighting it out on the other ship. Let the two drift apart. With the merchant crew still occupied in hand-to-hand fighting, you can turn your cannons on their ship at your leisure. Smash apart its hull until there is no doubt that it will sink. When it does, it will carry your zombies down with it.

Doing this two or three times ought to rid you of the "flotsam" zombies who have been crowding each other in the hold of your ship, waiting for their chance to enjoy deck-to-deck combat. It will not, however, rid you of your higher-functioning and specialized zombies. As it turns out, you'll need this (literal) skeleton crew for the next part of your retirement project.

Whereas pirates frequently retire by faking their own deaths and/or disappearing, you will ensure a secure retirement by **faking your own life.** What that means is this: You're far too famous a figure in the Caribbean to suddenly just disappear. People would be alarmed by your absence. Fleets from every port would scour the seas to learn what became of you (and your incredibly valuable hoard of treasure). You're also too competent and expert a pirate captain for the powers-that-be to "buy it" if you just float your ship into the Port-au-Prince harbor and have it suddenly explode. (A veteran sea captain like you would never allow a fire in your powder room to rage out of control.) True, you might stage a nautical battle in which a bounty hunter "defeats" you, but people are going to want proof. The word of a bunch of sailors that they defeated "the famous zombie pirate captain" just isn't gonna cut it. People will want to see your head on a pike. (Further, if you involve confederates in your charade, there is every chance that one of them who feels underpaid or underappreciated will decide to spill the beans.)

No, you need to create the impression that **you're still out there,** sailing the high seas and biding your time before you strike again. You need a continuation of your life without you (or, at least, your life as a pirate). To create the impression that you remain on the hunt, you must train your skeleton crew to sail in circles around the Caribbean while never actually pulling into port or engaging another ship. This will be easier to do than you might think. A high-functioning zombie helmsman still remembers how to grip the ship's wheel, knows to turn it occasionally, and retains the impression that running into land or rocks or other ships is bad to do. After a few instructions, you can set him loose and watch him go.

Because your ship will still be seen sailing around, nobody will suspect that you have gotten out of piracy. Other ships may sight yours, but they will not need to see you personally pacing the deck to know who you are. If other ships try to engage yours, your zombie helmsman will naturally take evasive action. (While some onlookers will be puzzled as to why you would flee—when previously you *always* stayed and fought—nobody will guess that it's because you're not onboard anymore.)

Once you've set your zombie helmsman to sail on this course for eternity, get into a dinghy with a couple of your best zombies and have them row you away. Specifically, have them row you to a port where you can—in disguise and under an assumed name—purchase a nondescript ship that you can then use to go around and collect all your buried treasure.

You want an all-zombie team for this operation. Revealing the location of buried treasure and digging it up is some of the most dangerous work there is to be had in the Caribbean. Many pirates have been known to execute the workers who help them bury or exhume their ill-gotten gains. In your case, just using your remaining zombies should do the trick. **Don't involve any other humans.** You may wish to leave at least a couple of treasure chests buried, just for insurance. (They say that gold is a "hedge against the future." If that's true, then buried gold is like a hedge against a hedge. Nothing could be more secure than properly buried treasure. Even retired pirates have rainy days.)

Once your treasure has been collected and stowed aboard your new boat, you can sail for lands uncharted—or at least someplace where people haven't seen you before—and make a new home. Direct your zombies to carry your treasure ashore, then return them to the sea where they can join your pirate ship and sail in perpetuity. (You may be tempted to keep a couple of zombies in your personal retinue. Certainly, they make awesome butlers and gardeners, but this can be a risky move. If somebody notices that your groundskeeper is more than a little bit "undead looking," people are going to start asking questions.) Buy yourself a nice house and settle into your new life. Just be sure to create a new persona that accounts for your vast wealth. You can be a banished duke or member of a deposed royal family, a roaming industrialist, or an eccentric inventor. ("You know those corsets that strap women in so tight that their internal organs shift? Yeah, I invented those.") Just make sure nothing about you says "ex-pirate." Sword and bullet wounds should be covered at all times. Beards should be shaved or at least trimmed into commonly accepted styles. If you must wear an eye patch, make a point to choose one that's not black and decorated with an embroidered skull and crossbones.

By retiring carefully and cautiously and avoiding the pitfalls that usually ensnare those who have dealt in zombies and dabbled in piracy, you can live long enough to enjoy your spoils.

Final Thought

You've Got the Tools, Now Go For It!

Like I said back at the beginning, it's a tough world out there. Opportunities for advancement aren't exactly coming at you thick and fast. You've got to make your own magic happen. And what is the Caribbean if not a place of magic? Here are found voodoo and piracy and zombies and murder and vast sums of plundered money and treasure.

Only those willing to take bold steps will actually obtain the riches of the Caribbean that so many seek.

Pirates are a dime a dozen. So are zombies. Just as two otherwise uninteresting chemical elements can be combined to create a terrific reaction, so can pirates and zombies be

247

united to create a dynamic force that can hunt the seas like no one has before.

Is raising a zombie pirate crew difficult? Yes. Is it complicated? Absolutely. Does it entail special risks? You know it does!

It also entails special rewards.

Through the difficult, tedious, and dangerous combination of zombies with piracy, one can also rise to the pinnacle of the outlaws' career, becoming the ultimate force for plunder in the Caribbean. Yours will be a crew that sails day and night, never resting until your appetite for treasure is sated.

Look, I mean you've already come **this** far. Why **not** take the final step? You're already in the Caribbean. You're familiar with zombies, and half your drinking buddies are probably pirates. Clearly, you're interested in being in exciting places where the extralegal is not only possible but also sort of accepted.

Why not become a part of that excitement? Why not become the **center** of it?

Remember, unlike a zombie, you only live once.